Transitioning from a shattered heart

Part 1

Darshini Devi Ramsaran

Dedication:

I thank God the almighty for guiding me through the difficult times, for giving me hope, for showing me that at the end of every dark tunnel there is a bright light awaiting my presence. Thank you God for your gift of knowledge, wisdom, love, compassion, and loyalty. I am who I am because of you and I thank you for everything.

My mother Mohanie, my father, Mahadeo. My grandmother Doris. My brothers, Seunauth, Hansraj, Satish, my sister in laws, Jaime, and Sherien. My nieces, Brittany, Sarah, Ariel, and Alexandra. My nephews, Michael, Tyler, Brandon, Solomon, Jacob, Mason, and my niece's husband Jose. My aunts, uncles, and cousins. Melissa, Rosa, Gracie, Mariam, Mariah, Vanessa, Lisa, Tiffany, Melissa D, Eva, Sabrina, and the many more special women who have been such a blessing and guide in my life. A special dedication to my lawyers, Avideh, Caroline, and my instructor Angelo from Sanctuary for families. I would also like to thank Governor Paterson for my pardon and allowing me to stay in the United States Of America. I do not know where my life would been without your special time and dedication into my education, my freedom, and my safety. I would also like to thank those who have been a lesson in my life, Derrick, Rajin, Vickram, you have all been a lesson learnt. I thank God for showing me that I was worth more than the verbal, sexual, financial, and mental abuse from each of you. I would like to thank my husband Navindra for pushing me to accomplishing my goals and supporting my journey. I love all of you very much and I am ever grateful for this opportunity and the impressions each of you have left in my heart. Thank you.

This Book is based on some fiction and non fiction. It is filled with lots of emotions; suspense, thriller, twisted relationships, verbal, physical, sexual and financial abuse, betrayal, and lots of inspiring poetry.

This Book's purpose is to ensure that there is hope, no matter what trials we may face, what battlefield we are on, which direction we are going, and where we came from, we should never lose sight of our purpose on this Universe. Each of us have a purpose, my purpose is to ensure my readers that if I overcame they can and will too. My purpose is to help in healing others that have experienced the same or similar situations I have been through, with messages in my writings. Life is full of ups and downs, rain and sunshine, happiness and sad, good and bad, innocent and evil... whatever it may be we are here for a reason. This book may give you the courage and strength to face what may come, the faith to stand strong and firm to get through the storms, and the motivation to accomplish your goals.

Poetry

Poetry is about
It is wanting to resurrect or preserve or do things that pull
against the fact of our mortality
Accepting criticism gracefully
Let your subconscious do the writing.
Edit carefully and without judging your own creativity.
You can write short sweet and simple
Or long heartbroken memories
The beauty of poetry is that you get to decide in your mind what
you comprehend.
With time and persistence
Dedication and motivation
Writing becomes easier and the words flow faster
The emotions grow deeper and life feels less painful as a weight
lifted off your shoulders
Poetry is to inspire and be inspired
It is to define the world, life, families, friends, music, love, hate,
husbands and wives, parents, grand parents, ancestors, children,
rape, education, work, in laws, fun, sex, money, abuse, drugs,
alcohol, etc…
Poetry can be written in many forms
And about anything
If you sit in silence and meditate on your title
You will find words that connects with another creating sentences
and paragraphs, to pages and books.
Poetry is about
Digger deeper
Reaching for your soul
The hidden words which describes your emotions at the moment
Love

Hate

Gain

Lose

Pain

Inspiration

Hurt

Blame

Energy draining

Realize

Experience

Expectations

Anger

It's beautiful to connect words and bring fourth

Smiles

Tears

Anger

Help

Advice

Trust

Loyalty

Relationships

Destruction

Business

Family

Career

And so much more

So the next time anyone has agreed to disagree

With the things I write

I hope you understand

That with poetry

It soothes the soul

Melts the heart

And changes your perspective on things through the eyes of the
writer
He/she captures your personality
And embeds it into their heart
The way that poem makes them feel after reading it
A precious memory that would last for all of eternity

"When tragic experiences occurs in our lives, we can either challenge it and face it straight on, or we can dismiss it and runaway; only to find ourselves reliving the same experience in our heads over and over. That is our choice of free will; which would you choose?"

However,

While running, we never truly have escaped, nor healed past the hurt, we tend to brush it under the rug in hopes of it never resurfacing, yet it always comes back, in many many ways or forms. Ways of which we don't understand and that is with the patterns in every choice we make, and in forms of who we choose to allow in our space.

Life has a cycle and a phase. What occurs within us emanates outwards. What you sow, is what you reap. If you plant seeds of positivity, you will bloom into someone magnificent. If you sow seeds of negativity, you will always attract just that.

Feeling sorry for yourself will attract those who also feel sorry for you and then it becomes their stepping stool in diminishing you; because they have found your weakness. If you protect your energy and raise your vibrations through positivity, then no matter which road you choose to take, you will always survive.

Writing & its powers

Writing & it's powers
One day I pray to become the most important writer in the universe
Creating a different story for the eyes of many to read along the white blue lined pages
I pray that my writings teaches love, compassion, and things in which many are able to relate to
Past, present, & future
Speaking into existence life or death
I pray my writing takes others on levels they never imagined they could be on
Levels higher above their own understandings
I pray my words speaks through the heart and it's desires of a better place
I pray that each word written by my hands ignites the fire in your burning desires
That gates open and reveals the purity of my life in front your eyes as you devour into the meanings behind those lines
I hope that the sun continues to shine although rainy days I prefer but for my readers I wish they are sunny and bright

inhaling the morning light exhaling the darkened cold and lonely nights

As each page takes you through a different universe

Speaking and pronounced differently each letter as it rolls off the tip of your tongue

I pray that you inhale and exalt my name

As I take you through some of memory lane

Although you may shed a tear from time to time

Let me clarify that though tears at night joy cometh in the morning light

Peace can be with you as you heal past and push through

Levels of pain leads you through life's knowledge as gained

I pray my writings break those walls which you built around yourself to let go and let God do the rest

I pray I break that barrier between healing and hurt and combine them both to understand their points

I pray that each weak point is renewed with strength and more driven for progress of the hearts healing

Through my writing you will

See who

I am and begin to believe in yourself first and know that power comes with the choices of your words

PROLOGUE

Run.

She gasped for air. Thoughts ran through her mind to run and, keep running, never to look back nor return. The only problem is that she was out of breath, shivering from the cold crisp air, her body was bruised internally, and externally, she was dehydrated, and haven't eaten in days. Samaya, a twelve year old girl who lost a little of her sanity in just a few minutes of a culprits sick, twisted desires of raping a young girl. She was his victim. Days went by as her mind slowly deteriorated, she lost all hope, all sense of direction, and her faith in God. She became the talk of the town, as friends and families began to make her feel judged based on their facial expressions. She started having suicidal thoughts, began cutting her arms, overdosing on medications, cutting school, following the wrong company, dating the wrong guys, running away from home, ending up in the psychiatric ward, and then ended up in jail.

Keep reading to find out more of Samaya's Transitioning from her shattered soul...

Forced to kill by the devils whisper in my ear
The devil whispers in my ear

Forced to live and escape mentally my being
To rule over the lifeless body which sits in front of me while I
held that scalpel in my right hand
All sorts of thoughts ran through my head
Invading the tiny space of sanity of which I had left
I am forced to make a decision quickly
Soon the cops will
Flood this facility
and the thoughts remain the same
"Should I let his lifeless body bleed out slowly or should I rip
through his body again and again until I'm certain that he is
dead?"
Time ticking as the first instinct I came up with
Rip through as that body turns blue, and pale
Knowing I've drained every drop of blood out of his disgusting
veins
I'm satisfied now
He won't ever get to touch any other little girl again
Inappropriately
He wouldn't be alive to penetrate his penis inside a twelve year
old child
I am forced to stop him now while I can
the devils whispers in my ear
Take the life of those who don't deserve
Your wish
my command
It was all just a thought...

Chapter One
The Rape

November 12, 1997

Walking along the sidewalk on a cold winter night as the snowflakes descends through the dark black skies, ten degrees outside, as the tears flows uncontrollably from my eyes, staining my cheeks with each drop as it freezes before it can fall on the floor. I've been walking these streets with the same stained up clothes for the past two days, trying to find my way home. I was afraid and all alone. I had no trust in anyone and I was losing my sanity a little each second that passed. I wasn't sure wether I was going or coming anymore. At the age of twelve, battling with diabetes, and a thyroid condition and then this...

This is my story,

Trains passing one after another, horns honking as I walked underneath the overpass and across the two way street of Fulton Avenue, not looking for any signs of distraction but only to what was ahead of me, a blank white wall as my feet takes me there but my mind is elsewhere. I hear the noises but I was a blank page at that moment. I can still hear myself screaming but no voice coming out, my stomach doing somersaults as I tried to push off but no strength in my arms, my body laid still and numb. I was furious and hurt. My eyes kept trying to force its way to open although my mind was telling me to block it out with eyes closed. I tired to go into a zone and just let it be over with already, but I fought through to see the face of the culprit which forced his way on top of me. I had to see so I will never forget, and at that instant I promised myself, that one day I will get through this, and one day I will get my revenge. I was only twelve years old at that time and I was a very good innocent child. I was loved by my family and friends, I didn't do any harm to anyone and so I wondered why me?

As I continued to walk, I remembered waking up in between the force which was upon me draining my energy and devouring my spirit, turning me into a walking zombie. I was fully awoken the following morning and all I saw was the bloody stained sheets which I laid on, in the old attic apartment. I got off the bed and stumbled on a box of children toys, my eyes began to look around, I began to scream help me, someone please help me! No sight of anyone, no sounds, but there was a stench; a mixture of stale dried and fresh blood. I presumed towards the stairs leading me to the lower level of the house, as I got to the bottom of the stairs I saw a friend of mine laying in the arms of a man on the beige sofa bed. I wondered what happened to her, and so I decided to wake her up as quietly as possible. Her name is Shelly. Shelly, began to scream at me and tell me grow up when I asked her to leave with me before she gets hurt. I tried to tell her that I was raped, but from the anger in her voice of me waking her up was so harsh I decided to walk out by myself, wobbling through the doors and that was when I heard her laughter as well as the man whose arms she laid in.

I tried to recap what actually occurred that night prior to me getting raped and what might have caused it. I had so many questions in my mind and no one that I can ask. Those who I thought were my friends was actually my enemies, prowling and contemplating in ways of destroying me. I was betrayed by that friend named Shelly. Then it dawned on me, bits and pieces started coming back to me. After I did a long cultural, religious dance in the temple for the Hindu religious holiday, (Diwali) Shelly and I decided to walk home. It was almost 10:30 pm that night when we left the temple, so Shelly insisted in me walking with her to her uncle job and have him take us both home. At first I was hesitant but I eventually agreed and carried along with her as we laughed and talk about school projects coming up, how perfect I played Mother Laxmi (Hindu goddess), about me becoming the best Doctor one day, as she explained she wasn't sure yet what she wanted to be as of yet. We had a great walk filled with lots of talks and laughter. Finally, we got in front of Shelly's uncle job. It was a bar and lounge. At twelve years old I didn't know what that was, nor was I ever exposed to any of the sort of environment prior to this day. We proceeded inside and waited as Shelly's uncle told us to. While we were waiting, a female brought Shelly and myself two cans of coca cola soda, and at first I refused because my mother always taught me to never accept anything to eat or drink from strangers, but of course Shelly was my friend and I trusted her when she said it was okay for me to accept it because, that is her uncle and he would never do anything to hurt neither one of us. I didn't realize I was so thirsty until I drank the whole can within a short space of time. I remembered getting a severe headache few minutes after I had the soda. First thing that came to my mind is that I am a diabetic and maybe my sugar levels were too high. I got very dizzy and I fell. I couldn't remember anything other than waking up and passing out on and off on a strange bed, in a strange place with a stranger on top of me, with my hands and feet tied down at the corners of the bed.

As I continued to walk, the tears kept flowing, my body began to tremble, I was weak, starved, dirty and afraid. I had no friend or family I wanted to trust to tell. I had no way to call for help because I refused to ask anyone for their help. If my own friend could put me in a predicament like that just imagine what a stranger would do. I just kept walking in search of my home, but each turn I made, I was lost, I was confused and I kept having flash backs of that night. I just wanted to curl up and die. I was ashamed of myself, I hated me after that! My innocence was gone. I was used up and abused. I suddenly felt the hands of someone on my arms when stopped in the middle of the road, and when I turned around it was my aunt. My aunt Theresa grabbed me and started screaming at me for running away, but when she told me to look her in the eyes and answer her, she saw the tears in my eyes as I was speechless and stuck and all I saw was her lips moving and no sound to my ears after that. Once again, I blanked out! My aunt took me home and she told my mom to call the cops and get an ambulance to come take me to the hospital. My aunt saw the blood on my clothes and asked my mother to not look at me and not say anything at all. Of course my mother didn't listen and she demanded to see my condition because, after all she is my mother and I am her only daughter.

My relationship with my mother was not the best but it sure wasn't the worse. My mother has always been my protector, director, teacher, and much more. She always told me "let me be your mother, your sister and your best friend". My biggest problem with my mother was not being able to trust that whatever I say to her would just stay between us and no one else. My mother has dealt with depression since a child and her way of coping with it was talking it out to her family and I know that it is good if she only told family but, in all honesty I didn't like it. It then became like hell for me. I had aunts, uncles, cousins, their friends, pastors, whom ever that were close to my family giving me their speeches, either yelling at me, or trying to control me. With all of this said, my mother was still my everything. She was always the woman I run to, the woman with a heart of gold and forgiveness, the woman of strength and dignity, my mother has always been my biggest supporter, advisor, and inspiration. She took one peak at me and started to scream "my baby" and cried until she fainted.

The sounds of sirens was all I heard after my mother screams. I passed out! And, when I awoke a doctor was by my side with a needle piercing my skin, and an oxygen mask on my face.i started panicking and asked the nurse "how did I get here"? "The ambulance brought you in, you are inside of Queens General Hospital located in Queens, New York, and your family is in the waiting room". Nurse Vixen replied.
Slowly, and steady I raised my body to an upright position, sitting with my back against the pillow and my face towards the door. The room began to get crowded with officers, hospital staffs, and a therapist, and each one of them had questions one after another.
I was forced to keep repeating what occurred that night, each time I was interviewed by someone different. It was extremely hard for me to keep talking when I had severe pains in my abdomen, my wrists, ankles, and the soles of my feet. I was bruised inside and out.

The doctors came in and explained to me that I had endured trauma to the right side of my head, a slight brain hemorrhage, and excessive internal bleeding, also that they found a date rape drug in my blood results. With everything occurring all at the same time and having to repeat myself, on top of all these complications, it made me angry. I just wanted to be left alone. I just needed sleep. I went into a state of delusion and thought it was all just a huge nightmare. At least that was what I wanted it to be. I tried to block out my surroundings and lose myself in a dark silent hole, where no one existed, no questions to answer, and no yelling in my ears. Sure enough, I was never left alone to go into my own world.

"Ms. Samaya Ray, I am Doctor Joesph and I would like for you to schedule an appointment with me for the starting of your therapy, when would you like to come"? Asked Doctor Josep.

"I am not sure, as my mind isn't here at the moment and I would like some time alone for myself please. Until then, kindly excuse me" I replied.

"That is absolutely fine, but do not hesitate for long because, dramatic experiences can lead to long term depression and possibly suicidal thoughts. This is my card, feel free to contact me at any time." Stated Doctor Joseph.

"I appreciate your advice doctor, however, I already feel like that and there isn't anything anyone can do to change that besides me. Seeing a psychiatrist, taking medications, and doing group therapy isn't for me. I do not want to be a walking zombie nor do I have anything to say to a complete bunch of strangers. My trust is like walking into a dead zone. Now, please leave before I get disrespectful" I screamed!

"I will leave my card with the front desk if you decide to change your mind" He replied.

"Have a good day" I replied.

"You as well, Ms.Ray"

Mr. Joseph, was only trying to help but, I didn't want to listen. I was exhausted and just wanted to be left alone. The air condition was on full blast and I barely had any covers over me. I was shivering and my eyes were swollen and blood shot red. I was unable to remember when was my last meal, shower, brushed my teeth, combed my hair, or changed my clothes. I got up and went to the bathroom for some peace and quietness. Sure enough I was interrupted by a knocking at the door.

"Knock, Knock"
"knock, knock, knock"

I can hear someone banging on the bathroom door, while my back was against the other side of that door and my buttocks on the floor. Knees to my chest, head bent downwards, and both hands on the sides of my head, as my mind drifted into a dark tunnel with no escape. I became a prisoner within my mind and thoughts.
Eventually, I decided to open the doors and came out of the bathroom to get the questions out of the way. I figured the faster I get it out the way, the faster I can go back into my dark tunnel and try to figure out where I fit in this world.

"Ms.Ray, I am Detective Jones, I have been assigned your case, and I have a few questions for you. Would you mind giving me answers to the best of your knowledge"?

"Yes, sure" I replied.

"Can you tell me what day and time you last remembered when this incident occurred"? He asked.
In disbelief, he just jumped straight to the point.

"Yes, it was November 12, 1997 between approximately eleven o'clock pm to twelve midnight". I answered.

"What was the last thing you remembered before you arrived at the hospital"? He questioned.

"I remembered my mother screaming and crying" I replied.

"Who is Shelly"? He asked with a stern voice.

From his facial expression and the tone of his voice I assumed he was agitated with the sound of her name.

"Shelly, was a friend of mine" I stated.

"Was, a friend of yours, meaning what exactly"? He asked.

"i believe that Shelly set me up for this to happen, because the last conversation I had with her was a blank to me, however I did remember her laughing while I was trying to escape that strange place."

And just like that I blurted out how I felt. I accused her immediately! My gut feeling was pointing all fingers on her based on the reaction she gave me; rather than her helping me, she ridiculed me.

"Do you remember what this guy looked like?" He questioned.

"Yes, he is about 5 feet, 6 inches tall, yellow skin complexion, right side nose piercing, short buzzed hair cut, and about 160-170 pounds".

And the questions went on, one after another until the tears began to flow from my eyes, and finally I got the break I needed so badly.

"That is all for now Ms.Ray, if I have further questions, I will be reaching out to you. In the meantime, I wish you well, and a fast healing. Here is my card, If there is anything you do remember and would like to add in addition to the case, which you may find resourceful in any way to catching this culprit, do notify me". Detective Jones stated.

"Will do Detective, and thank you". I replied.

"No need to thank me, it is my job". He said. He began to walk out the door and turnt back sighed, then smiled and looked me in the eyes.

"You will get through and past this one day, and I promise to find that dirt bag who did this to you" he stated, in a furious, and angry tone.

I could see in his eyes that he was hurt. I felt his energy, and it led me to believe that he meant every word he spoke. I knew that Detective Jones would do whatever it took to make sure he was the one to make that arrest. Although knowing this, it didn't make me feel any better. I wanted to find that rapist and cut him limb by limb and pour acid over each part of his body, while he watches me as I do it. I wanted revenge, but I also wanted to die.

"Ms.Ray, I am Doctor Sylvia, I will be determining your release, based on your mental and physical health."

"Okay"I replied.

After a full physical examination and Doctor Sylvia has properly reviewed documents from the psychiatrist, I was told to follow up with psych therapy, as well as an OBGYN, and the detectives. I was required to take eight hundred milligrams of Ibuprofen, for any pains or muscle spasms.

"Thank you Doctor". I responded.

I slowly got off of the hospital bed and began to put on the clean clothing which my mother left for me with the Doctors for when I got released. I started to get severe cramping in my abdomen, but I didn't speak up about the pains because I knew I would be stuck in there for much longer than expected. I clenched my teeth and cringed through the aches and eventually managed to get dressed.

When I walked through the exit door, I saw both my parents, my three brothers and my aunt. They were all in tears with their faces peered to the door for my exit.The sight of their faces made my heart ache much more than what I was already going through. I had to face them regardless and I had to find the courage somehow, so I wiped my tears and showed them signs of aggression rather than pain. The entire drive home was quiet. I didn't speak, they didn't question; there were only sobs and sniffles. When my father arrived in front of the house, I quickly got out of the vehicle and asked my mother for her keys to open up the door and I ran inside. I went straight towards the bathroom. Before I walked into the bathroom there was a closet door to the left of me, which contained cleaning products. I opened the door and retrieved a gallon of bleach and presumed to the bathroom. I got in the shower and started scrubbing my body with bleach and soap until my skin turned bright reds and purples. I can feel the cuts blistering as the water runs on my body. I scrubbed so hard that I had tiny open wounds all over my body.

"Knock, knock"
"Who is it?" I yelled.

"It's me".My mother responded.

I got out of the shower and opened the door for my mother. I couldn't hold back the tears any longer. When my mother entered the bathroom, she closed the doors behind her and before I could get back in the shower she grabbed my arms and pulled my 100 pound soaking body close to her and hugged me tightly. She was hysterical.

"I will always be here for you. I want you to know that whenever you are ready to talk to me I will be here to listen. I am sorry this had to happen to you. I tried to protect you and warn you about friends and now look what happened. I will kill that Bitch Shelly if I ever see her again. I don't care if I go to jail". My mother furiously stated.

"Mom, I honestly don't want to discuss this anymore. I am disgusted in myself for not listening to you in the first place. I know that was wrong of me, but I don't think I should be reminded about it over and over". I replied to her statement.

"I understand, go shower and I will be here if you need my help". My mother explained.

I got back in the shower with the assistance of my mothers hand guiding me.

Finally, after so many days I was able to feel a little less dirty. I got out of the shower and began to walk towards my room. That was when my father was walking in my direction and looked me in the eyes with tears streaming down his face, he was unable to speak; his mouth was fumbling for words and eventually he walked away and went out the door. It was hard for my loved ones to see me in that state of mind and condition. I didn't care to speak to any male figures; wether it be my brothers or dad, uncles or guy friends, they all were the same in my eyes. That was a very hurtful moment between a father and daughter. I couldn't begin to imagine what my parents were going thorough. The more I saw them at their weakness the more distant I tried to be. That same night mother came to my room to say goodnight while I was lost in deep thoughts.

"Can you hear me?"My mother began to question.

I didn't realize she has been talking the entire time until she shook me by my shoulders and questioned again

"Did you hear anything I said"?

"No, mother I didn't" I explained.

"I said please take all the time you need but I think you should give Doctor Joseph a call as earlier as possible. You need someone to talk to if not your family". She began to explain.

"Yes, mother I will. Please, let me get some sleep" I pleaded.

"Okay, goodnight. I love you"!

"I love you Mother" I responded.

I wish there was a way to make all of this disappear, I thought to myself. That night I tossed and turned in fear, and pain. Finally, sleep caught up with me and I knocked out; around 3 o'clock that following morning, my mother ran in my room because she heard screaming coming from my room. I was having nightmares of that night. My mother, the gentle hearted woman that she is, cradled me in her arms and soothe me with her singing, right back to sleep.

I woke up about 10 am that morning and came out of my room to brush my teeth and take a shower. "Good Morning, sis" my little brother Amit said.

"Good Morning" I replied.

I lowered my head in disgust of myself, and carried on to the bathroom. After I was finished my morning rituals, I got on the phone and called Doctor Joseph, as I promised my mother.

"Good Morning, Doctor Joseph office. How may I direct your call"? Questioned the receptionist.

"Good Morning, My name is Samaya Ray, and I am calling to make an appointment or a possible walk in to speak with Mr. Joseph". I Explained.

"Yes, Ms.Ray, you are welcome to walk in today if you like".

"I will be there for 1 pm if that is okay"

"Yes, that is fine, seen you then"

I got dressed as quickly as I could and headed out the door. While waiting on the bus, my dad pulls up in the car and tells me he will take me. I felt awkward but I got in the car and kept silent the whole ride to the Doctor office. He nor I spoke a word until I got in front of the office.

"Call me when you are finished, I will be around the area to take you back home". My dad said.

"Okay" I responded.

"Good Afternoon, Ms.Ray. Please come with me" Doctor Joseph called

"Have a seat Ms.Ray. Please understand that whatever you say to me is completely confidential. The only time I will ever have to disclose any information you tell me is if I find you in any form of danger to yourself or others. Now, let us begin".

"Ms.Ray, would you like to start out by telling me more about yourself?" He Questioned.

"What would you like to know?" I asked.

"Lets start out with, what is your favorite color, what do you like to do with your free time, or what are your hobbies?"

"My favorite color is blue, I like to read, write, draw or make things with my hands".I answered.

"Okay, that is a great start"

"Doctor Joseph, I don't see what this has to do with my therapy"I explained.

"Ms.Ray, this has nothing to do with your therapy sessions. I am getting to know you for the person you are, the things you like or dislike so that the sessions will flow smoothly. I would like to take this opportunity to allow you to introduce yourself as well as I will do the same". He explained.

"Okay, what else would you like to know"? I questioned.

"Tell me about your family, your friends, your school, goals, etc…"

I began to give him a full introduction of myself and my life prior to the rape. He sat and listened without interrupting and I was able to open up a little. I was a bit unsettled at first because he is a man after all and I was a bit scared to be behind closed doors talking to him after that dramatic experience I went through. I scheduled another meeting with him for the following week although I didn't want to but; I did it because I was not able to go back to school as of yet and the visits with my doctors as well as therapist were the only connection I had to the outside world.

Week three of my session, while I was inside of Doctor Joseph's office, we were interrupted by a knock on the door.

"Good afternoon, Doctor Joseph. Good afternoon, Ms.Ray. I am here to ask you to come with me down to the precinct to pick out the culprit from our line up". Asked Detective Jones.

"Sure" I agreed immediately.

"Ms.Ray, we will continue same time on Wednesday, good luck to you and remember what we discussed. Have a beautiful day". Stated Doctor Joseph.
"Thank you" I replied.

"Have a good day Doctor" Detective Jones said.

I sat in the back seat of the Detective car, as my hands, feet and face began to accumulate sweat. My nerves were shot. I was nervous but at the same time relieved. I prayed that he was in that line up although prayers was the last thing I wanted to do. I wanted a sweet revenge.
We arrived...

"Ms.Ray, just follow me". Detective asked.

We continued walking down the corridors, through two doubled metal doors, and down two flights of stairs.

"Ms.Ray, I want you to take your time in identifying each individual".

I entered a room with a window and behind that window stood six guys. I jumped backwards because I was afraid of them seeing me.

"Do not worry, Ms.Ray. if you are worried that they can see you, don't be. This is a window which allows you to see them but on their end, it seems as a black window and they cannot see in this room at all" Detective Jones assured me.

I began walking across the room looking each one in the face and immediately stopped when I got to the fourth guy in the lineup. I froze in that position, just staring at him, with evil thoughts in my head. I was interrupted when I heard a voice yelled on the intercom.

"Fourth person, please step forward" The Detective asked.

He began to walk closer to the window and my heart began to race, my veins felt like they were about to explode, and I began to sweat. I could feel my anger rising.
"Ms.Ray, I need you to take a closer look at the remaining individuals in the line up to make sure" said the Detective

"I don't need to"! I yelled.
"I will never forget that disgusting face"!

"Officer Linder, please bring the fourth individual out to the basement for fingerprinting and allow the remaining to go"Asked Detective Jones.

"Will do, Sir" Replied Officer Linder.

I watched the culprit being escorted out of the room, and I pushed through the doors on the opposite side to face him, to spit on him, to attack him, but I was stopped by a few officers. I just wanted to show that disgusting man that I wasn't afraid of him. I wanted him to worry about my next move. I wanted to put fear in his heart. Unfortunately, I was not granted my hearts desire. I left the police station with a little bit more of a relief yet somehow my spirits were unsettled. I felt like jail wasn't supposed to be his punishment. It should have been much more. Possibly death!
But then I thought, death would make it much more simple for him, and so my thoughts kept drifting into other ways of inflicting pain on him as he did to me. I wanted to cut his penis out and shove it in his buttocks, slice him to tiny pieces while he was still breathing.

"Ms.Ray, I am Officer Luna, I will assist you to getting home safely" she stated.

"Okay, thank you" I replied.

I got a ride home with a female officer from the station after the perpetrator was secured behind the cell. The entire ride she was trying to convince me that I will get through this tragic experience. I just sat in silence and listened.

"We're here Ms.Ray". Stated Officer Luna

"Thank You, ma'am" I said.

"You are very welcome my dear" she replied.

I closed the car door and walked towards my house.
I got to the front door and decided to sit on the front stairs for a little while, and clear my mind. My brother interrupted my train of thoughts a few moments after I sat down.

"Sis, do you want anything from the pizzeria or the Chinese restaurant?" Amit questioned.

"No, I am okay thanks"

"Are you sure"? He questioned again.

"Yes, I am sure" I replied.

I watched him walk out the gate with a sad face. It was over three weeks already and I was unable to associate myself with anyone other than authorities. I completely blocked everyone else out. I stayed by myself most of the time. I began writing more and more, ignoring the world and focusing on releasing this bottled up pain. My days felt longer and my nights felt shorter.

I wrote a poem:

I write with a passion
All within me

Deep intellectual conversations written into poetic form
Creating an illusion
Adorning the mind
Taking you on a roller coaster ride
Sometimes up, sometimes down

I write with a mind filled of invigorating thoughts
The imagination I create is magical in every aspect
It is a way to control the mind and force emotions upon an
individual
Bringing out things deep within the reader
Some may have experienced
Some may be curious
Some may cry
Some may smile
Some may laugh
But through it all
Words written with power in the hands which holds that pen
Seizing time and taking control
Of the eyes which glides across the written words on the white
blue lined pages

I write because it frees my soul from the negativity
Causing life to replay over and over like a melody stuck in ones
head
Words used to describe an emotion
Creating a beautiful connection
To the hearts and souls
Those young and old
Through life or death
These words must be heard

I write with dignity and pride
With love and joy
Sometimes tears in my eyes
I write to let the world know
That knowledge must be shared
It costs nothing to share
but in everything you have gained
Much more wisdom
Much more of life
Much more pain
Much more strife
Because in life there are battles in which we must face
Because without sunshine
There would be no rain
Without water trees could not grow
Without love there would be no hate
One hand washes another
And love leads to fate

I write because
One road leads to many destinations
In which paths one must choose
The question is
Right path or wrong path
Which one would you choose?

I write to share the pains of another
And expressed emotions
The joy of life
The beauty of family
The love of a friend
The marriages of many

The cold concrete cell walls
The metaled mental bars
The man on the bike
The woman in the rain
The rape at 12
The world which will one day end
Etc...
It is never just about me
I write of other situations
And many more other stories
I write with anger
I write with fear
I write with drama
And I write with tears

I write each day
To remind myself
That I am worthy of more than I think
I write to let go of built up anger
I write to control my mind when it triggers
I write this journey
With strength and dedication
I write
To bring me out of any dark situation
I write to free my mind
I write to free my soul

देवी

As time went by I eventually went back to school, and tried to put this behind me. I began to make friends. I got myself a job and began working after school. There was a trial going on and I continued seeing my therapist. I tried to find ways to motivate myself and keep a positive track. I began to find solutions rather than creating problems in my head. The more I focused on the positive things I began to heal.

Six moths later…

A phone call came in from the district Attorney office.

"Hi, My name is Brooks. I am the district attorney in charge of your case and I would like to set up an appointment with you to come in and discuss the case. When are you available to come in"? She questioned.

"I can come in whenever you need me to" I replied.

"How does this coming Monday sound at around 10 Am"?

"That is fine" I replied.

When I got out of work later that night I told my mother about the phone call which I received and my mother and I discussed that she will be going with me and standing by my side every step of the way. I was a little relieved about that. I barely had time to think about much because my time was so occupied with school, friends, work and therapy. There wasn't much time for me to drift off into another universe in my mind. I did however, found myself a little confused that entire weekend. Just when I though it was over, and I managed to block out that nightmare, I was reminded once again. Its like the more I got to healing the more set backs I had. I just wanted this to be over already.

Finally, the day has came!

We arrived at the District Attorney's Office at 9:30 Am that morning.

"Ms.Ray, I am Courtney, please have a seat" she said.

I laid my head on my mothers shoulders while we sat side by side and I asked her for her forgiveness for shutting her out of my emotions. We began to have a heart to heart conversation and then got interrupted.

"Mrs.Ray, I need you to kindly have a seat and only allow your daughter to come in for now. It is a matter of privacy. We will notify you when you can enter the room". Stated Mr.Brooks

I looked over at my mother with confusion in my eyes. I wanted her to go with me this time and now she couldn't. I felt so hurt and so was she. This time I needed her more than ever. I knew I was going to break down in tears again. Just the thoughts brings tears to my eyes and pain in my heart. She got up out of her seat and gave me a tight hug.

"It will be okay, just stay strong and take your time answering their questions. I love you and I will be right here when you come out". My mother explained.

"I love you mom" I replied.

"Have a seat Ms.Ray. First I would like to say thank you for coming in and cooperating with us. Now in this discussion, there will be several questions which may be very difficult for you to answer and some may make you relive what you went through. This isn't an easy task for anyone to have to go through this. Being a victim of rape is a mental challenge. If for whatever reasons you need to stop and take a break, do not hesitate in asking to do so. To your right is a glass and a pitcher of water if in the event you need to clear your throat, feel free to help yourself. Now before we start, do you have any questions for me"? He explained.

"No Sir, I do not" I responded.

"Well then, let us get started".

There were several questions making me relive that day, over and over. I kept taking breaks because I was extremely hysterical. Eventually they allowed my mother in the room to comfort me. After they started the damages they just threw me into my mothers arms. My mother began questioning why did they bring me there in the first place. And so Mr. Brooks began to explain.

"i brought your daughter in today because the perpetrator who was arrested for this crime, decided to take his case to trial.

What happens at a trial hearing is that the defendant can try to prove his side in front of a jury. What then happens is evidence is produced and if necessary your daughter may have to face him if she is brought to the stand for her statement and also possibly crossed examined. If the perpetrator loses trial he will be facing the maximum penalty". Explained the District attorney.

"I understand, thank you and have a nice day" My mother replied.

"You as well Mrs.Ray. And as for you Ms.Ray do continue to stay strong and positive and I will be looking forward to prepping you for trial".

I lowered my head with disgust.

Weeks went by after that and I continued my therapy, school and work, including prepping for trial. I got midway in my trial prepping and I just stopped. I couldn't handle the pain, the pressure, and having to constantly justify or prove anything while I was being crossed examined. Although it was just a prepping, the district attorney made sure that he treated me as if he was the defendants attorney, while having a comeback at everything I said. I felt like I was being prosecuted rather than being saved. It was beginning to turn me into a whole different person. I became more bitter, more hurt, and more scorned. I had to walk away and leave it alone. "I will catch him one day if he gets prosecuted or not" I mumbled under my breath.

Life is a funny funny place

Life is a funny funny place
We are born to die
We suffer to live
We ache and cry
We love and smile
We grow angry and hate
We love and get married
We bore children to teach
We are born to reproduce
We raise pets to be loyal
We are taught to be humble
We kill to eat
We plant to reap
We create electricity to bring fourth light
We create gasoline to cook our food over
We are each created uniquely
We make music
We write lyrics
We are observers
We are dictators
We are followers
We are leaders
We are successful
We are in poverty
We are blessed
We are stressed
We are made to empower and be empowered
We are made to conquer
We are made to destroy
Life is a funny funny place
We live to learn

We adapt to surroundings
We are created to be our own
We are taught to reciprocate a good deed
We live to enjoy and be merry
We live to be sad and diverse
We are companions
We are associates
We are executors
We are defenders
We are sociopaths
We are condemn
We rebuke
We praise
We are judged and we judge
We are convicted and we are sentenced
We are good and evil
Life is a funny funny place
We are destined to become someone
Someone to inspire, to influence, to inquire and reason with.
Someone to admire and acknowledge leaving behind a legacy.
Love is life and life is a funny funny place
We endure and we disperse
For every action is a reaction!
Agree to disagree
Life is a funny funny place

By; देवी

Two months later...

I was served with an order of protection. Above the letter wrote, "The People vs. Mr.Lakhan". There was a full order of protection for him to stay away. In addition I received a document stating that Mr.Lakhan was sentenced to 6 months in jail, with five years probation. After reading this, I was more furious than ever.

"Only six months? This is wrong on so many levels". I yelled.

I had no choice but to accept what the system did. I didn't trust anyone for sure at this point. I canceled all of my appointments with my therapist. I started back my daily routine without a therapist this time. I began to stay clear of everyone and everything that could possibly put me in a bad situation. I became tough. I started fighting back what wasn't right or didn't serve purpose to me. I didn't have the courage to talk about things anymore. I began arguing and disrespecting others.

Life took a twist...

I began to looked at life a whole lot different.

Twisted thoughts

Twisted thoughts
Collective objects
Sharp instruments that can cut though the veins smoothly
leaving no traces of ridged edges
I know now that the
Doctors won't be able to find the actual incisions unless it bleeds
through and the blood surfaces to the top of my skin
That is the only way they will know that I've sliced through my
veins
As I sit near the window sill
Looking out I see
The vultures of deep black
Ravens
The sign of death drawing near
The sun dims as the moon shadows over
Thunder and lightning yet no sign of rain heading near
As
Twisted thoughts enters my head
If I pierced through just a little more
I can implode the vein causing me to bleed out
Leaving my body dried out as if someone sucked the life out of
my lungs
And ripped out my beating heart
I imagine
How would the coroner write their report
Would it be suicide or just another victim to a brutal attack of
Twisted thoughts
Implicated by another individual
Would the news report on television state that "a young woman
who was filled with such love by others committed suicide
because she was still not happy?"

Or would the title on the front page leave everyone worrying because they believe that someone like me who enjoys life so much was
brutally attacked in her own home?
I wonder sometimes if I did commit suicide,
What would the world believe and the ones who knows me
How would they look at the frontlines of the newspaper while they sip on their morning coffee?
I wonder what would they feel?
As I sit
With twisted thoughts of dismembering my body parts because I am fed up of life that which I was never happy at all
Pleasing others before myself
Taking into consideration of other individuals and their feelings
I forgot myself
And now that I am far gone
I live on with twisted thoughts
To be continued…

Chapter 2
Teenage years...

I had two female friends, I couldn't decide which one was my bestie but I knew they both were like sisters to me; Melissa and Tiffany. We went to the same P.S.214 elementary schools and continued to the same Junior high school. When I started back junior high school, they were my go to persons to cry with. I began opening up to them about a lot of personal things in my life. The conversations between the three of us were deep, intense, and extremely long. We were all there for each other when we needed to vent or cry, and even made each other laugh uncontrollably at times. Through my elementary school years, and all of my junior high school I was battling with being picked on, having a skin condition (Acanthosis Nigricans), my religion, my long Indian hair, my height, my weight etc... The verbal abuse from some of my classmates turned into physical when someone of the kids knew about me being raped and having the cops involved. I became all kinds of horrible words. Of all my classmates and so called friends, Tiffany and Melissa were the ones who were always there no matter what anyone called me.

Our conversations were so long that sometimes we got carried away and ended up being late for our classes many times. When I needed to run away from my problems, they would be right by my side cutting school with me, going to the beaches or parks and just talk. It was a stress relief for me as well as them.

I began to get into trouble with my parents all the time after I started cutting school. I didn't know how to drop a load of pain on them again about my verbal and physical abuse at school.

They were already trying their utmost best in healing past what occurred to me. As time went by and my parents continued to try to discipline me, I became more rebellious. I began running away from home. I ran away from listening to their constant preaching and arguing between themselves. I couldn't handle their strictness because I was already damaged property; at least that is what I thought I was. There wasn't anything else they could protect me from. My mindset was, "I got over that and nothing else can happen that I won't get over or through". I felt too grown for my age and I just needed my space. No one could understand unless I pointed it out, but if I pointed it out, they would begin crying or start getting depressed. I didn't want anyones sympathy nor advice. I just needed their prayers but I refused to ask for that.

I blamed God for not saving me, when I was very dedicated into worship and prayers. I lived my life on "comes what may or go, I didn't care anymore". I had low self esteem and I was unable to participate in group projects, change into my gym clothes in front of other females, I was unable to speak about my feelings to any counselor, and I distanced myself from most. I ended up in a state of deep dark depression which lead me to a psychiatric ward for two weeks, where I continued my writings.

Darkness in the Asylum

Darkness in the Asylum
Walls closing in
Visions of things
Mind boggled, thoughts are lost
My feet began wandering
Eyes open; yet blind
The darkness and invasion luring me in

My privacy stolen from me
The hallways that hears my screams
Needle after needle piercing through my skin
Hair rapidly falling from my head
As if shaved with an invisible razor on a thread slowing pulling
with vicious force
Face drooped, skin hanging, caused from deprivation of food
Body bruised from the constant beating
Wrists with lined imprints of the shackles which locked me away
Punished for my eyes playing tricks on me
Medications forcefully injected into my veins
My body shivers and with constant pain
as tears streams down my face, while I write this scribe and
lower my head in disgust of the person I've become
Institutionalized because I see things which are not always there!
Is it my fault that the darkness is closing me in?
To be continued....

When I was released from the ward I went right back to school and I ended up having more guys as friends than females; which became a conflict of interest for my family. Instead of me staying away from boys, I got closer to many of them. I did that at first with the intent of getting to know what goes through a male individual mind, and I began to understand a lot. I became friends with more guys than girls because the females were only interested in what they were wearing and how good they looked. Tiffany and Melissa were beautiful young ladies and didn't need to worry how they looked or dressed because they were always well kept and so was I. We became the popular girls after a while and everyone wanted to be our friends.

We were like the three musketeers and inseparable. I lived directly across the street from Tiffany on Liberty avenue between Sheridan avenue and Grant avenue, and Melissa lived a few houses away from me and Tiffany lived through Grant avenue. We always saw each other on a daily basis, wether in school, before or after school and sometimes on weekends. Tiffany and Melissa both grew up without a father figure in their lives and their mothers were forced to be both parents to each of them. I was lucky to have both of mine.

Some days I would runaway to their houses and try to escape from my family. Sure enough, my parents and brothers always knew I would be at either of their homes and would come search for me. Sometimes I wouldn't want to eat what my mother cooked but what Tiffany mother did and so we would exchange our dinners at times. Tiffany's mother was my other mother growing up and my mother became hers as well.

Time went by through the struggles of school, parents, and personal conflicts...

Tiffany, Melissa and myself managed to graduate from I.S.302 junior high school with excellent grades. I was accepted to some very good high schools that had the nursing programs which I wanted to be in. My mother was a Nurse at the time and so I wanted to be just like her when I grow up. Of course, tragic experiences made me change my opinions of everyone, however I still had a heart that wouldn't allow me to stop caring for people. My mother

was always my inspiration. Her love and affection for people were priceless. She would tell me to learn to forgive, so I can move forward with a clean heart and mind.

Tiffany, Melissa and I went to separate high schools. It was even more difficult for me to start over in a new environment with new classmates, when I only had these two females by my side the entire time.

That summer before high school started, we spent as much time as we could together. I was heart broken and I was afraid to lose this sister bond which we shared because things began to change rapidly. Tiffany and Melissa had boyfriends and were allowed to date and I had only them. I was not going to be a third wheel in anyones relationship so I began finding things to do with my time again.

Ninth grade…

I started making new friends at Hillcrest high school. I began the nursing program and did my phlebotomy hands on in Queens General Hospital as an intern. My father owned his own taxi company directly opposite of the hospital, so he would drop me off in front of the school and pick me up to take me to my training. He would wait for me to finish and he would take me with him while I did my homework in the car as he drives to and from one location after another dropping and picking up his passengers. Although my dad owned the company he also worked as a taxi driver. We began having a father and daughter relationship. Some mornings when I would not want to go to school he would allow me and my brother to stay home, even though my mother would disagree. My father allowed me and my brother to do things which my mother never approved and my mother would allow me to do things my father would never approve. My brother and I knew who we can have our way with. My father would take us to school and if I said I wasn't well, he would keep me and drive cab all day with me in the car. He would proudly introduce me to all of his customers as his only daughter and how proud he was.

My father would get us breakfast consisting of mixed green salad, hard boiled eggs, tuna salad and cashews, with an orange juice or hot chocolate for me and a coffee for him. If I stayed all day with him, he would get us lunch as well. Sometimes pizza, halal food, west indian or burgers and fries with milkshakes. My father always gave me and my brother five to ten dollars every day. Each of us got the same amount. We were spoiled when it came to him giving us money.

I looked forward to those days with my dad when I didn't have the courage to face the day with a smile on my face. My dad made it comfortable for me through those moments and gave me everything I asked. He never liked when I would wear skirts to school so my mother would allow me to hide and put it in my book bag and I would change in school and change back when he would come to pick me up.

One evening we got home and things changed...

A phone call came in one day that my grandfather has passed and my mother would be required to attend his funeral because it was my grandfather wishes. My mother didn't have her travel documents and my grandfather's funeral was in Canada. My mother began to panic and she didn't know how she would get there to fulfill her fathers last wish. My uncle in Canada reached out to some people who had connections with bringing people illegally to and from the country. They contacted my mother the following day and stated they would be picking her up by 10 pm.

"Samaya and Amit, I need to talk to the two of you. Sit down". My mother said.

"Okay" both my brother and I responded together at the same time with curiosity in our minds.

"I want you both to know I love you very much and I will always love you no matter where I go or what happens"

From those words and the sound in her voice, I could feel the tears beginning to accumulate in my eyes. I looked over to my little brother and tears were already streaming down his face. He is the baby in the family and he was the most affectionate and loving one out of all the siblings. He hurts when my mother is hurt, or his friends. He was the innocent one.

"I have to leave tonight, it was a last minute decision I had two make. I know it will be hard but mommy promises you that she will come back. I don't know how long I will be there but I promise to call every day and talk to both of you". My mother explained.

I couldn't hold back the tears any longer. I begged and pleaded and promised to be a better child. I felt like I was losing my everything at that moment. Although I didn't tell my mother my secrets or anything about my life, she was always there to listen and knowing she was there was most important for me. I felt guilty of blocking her out of my life and pleaded my cause of needing her to stay.

"I do not have my immigration papers and I am sneaking into another country to see my father one last time. I don't know what can happen to me if I am caught but I want you to know that no matter what happens this will never change my love for none of my children. Wherever I am I will find a way to call.

Please forgive me for going but this is my fathers last wishes and I have to fulfill it, one day you will understand if anything ever happens to me or your father". She continued to explain...

I had to be tough not just for myself but for my little brother too. I wiped my tears away and hugged my mother and told her I love her and to hurry back. I assured her I would try my best and hold it together and be there for my brother as much as I can. Through the school years as I was picked on so was my brother. If I wasn't able to fight my own battles I would definitely fight his and always win. Sometimes he was ashamed I was his sister because I always embarrassed him when I jumped in and he was fighting another kid. I was overly protective about him. We went to the same elementary school and junior high. Everyone know me as his big sister but also as his protector. Some kids teased him about it and some cheered him on about me. Regardless of his feelings I always had his back in anything. I told him I'm always going to be here and mom is coming back soon to wipe his tears and give her a hug.

That night we all agreed to pull together as a family and my two older brothers and their wives including my father was a team. My mother kissed and hugged us tightly and cried before she left. I didn't know that this would be the last time I would see her for the next eight months...

My mother arrived, safely in Canada and called as she promised. She continued to call and cry each day afterwards. She attended her fathers funeral and although her presence was there her mind was only on us. She called right after the funeral and told us she would be back in two weeks. We were so excited and couldn't wait. We continued speaking to our mother each day until the day of her departure from Canada.

Two weeks later...

My mother was on a similar trailer which she crossed the border the first time going into Canada. Only this time she was returning to the U.S. The Border Patrol stopped the trailer she was in. The Border Patrol had the dogs searched the trailer. My mother together with a few other females and males were caught illegally crossing back to the U.S. Immigration officers were quickly notified by the Border Patrol. They held my mother for questioning. My little brother and I over heard the conversation between our elder brothers, our sister in laws and our father. After hearing this, I immediately called my aunts and uncles and asked if it was true. They didn't know how to lie to us and they told me the truth.

I stayed in contact with my aunts and uncles in Canada who had information since that point because my mother gave the officers her brother and sister number as an emergency contact, knowing that they will inform her husband or children about her location.

I couldn't begin to imagine what my mother was going through. finally, my mother was released after my uncle got my mother a highly paid attorney to get out of custody.

My elder brother Rick and his wife Sherry decided to take me and my brother to Disney World in Florida for a two week vacation leaving my father behind so we can clear our minds. When we came back from having so much fun we were faced with reality.

A reality which I just wanted to escape. So I fell off track and began acting out in hopes of my mother coming back and staying with us. It was getting harder because my father was drinking every weekend. He was more strict on me more than anything and I couldn't understand why because I didn't even do anything wrong. He started taking out his frustration on us and cursing for every little things. He started sending me to my aunt and uncle business to stay after school and he would work and then pick us up from there. My father didn't trust us home alone when it made no sense because we were six and seven staying in the house by ourselves, when they worked full time jobs and we went to and from school by feet every day which was about five blocks away.

His frustration made me run....

Everything in my life began to fall apart. Days turnt into weeks, weeks into months. I missed my mother.

I started following the wrong company and began drinking my dads alcohol. I was cutting school at least two days a week, then I wouldn't show for an entire week, then it turnt into weeks at a time. I went to school jams where there was alcohol, or recreational drugs. I became even more rebellious. My life was about hanging out and escaping reality. I couldn't take the pressure I was under. I didn't even have a full chance to properly heal and here I was a 15 year old taking on so much weight upon my shoulders. My brother got along with my aunt and uncle and cousins more than I ever did. I stayed to myself most of the time. I didn't care to be around because I was still ashamed of what happened to me and my mother wasn't here to defend me if they ever made me uncomfortable. Most days I was depressed and I was in search of being loved so badly that I began to fall weak and I turned into an alcoholic.

I was taking my diabetes and thyroid medications and I would drink liquor straight from the bottle, not realizing the effect it could have on me. I went to school some days with a bottle in my bag mixed with soda. I use to take out half of the bottle of liquor leaving the other half in the bottle and mixing with water so my dad doesn't find out. Some days I would go in my room and pass out without eating the whole day. I began to lose weight rapidly. My skin condition was getting worse and I didn't know why. Some days I wasn't even coming home from school. I would hang out all day at the park, and at night I would take the A Train to Rockaway beach and walk to 98 street. I found my peace by the waters no matter what I was going through. I would walk down and underneath the boardwalk and sit where just a tiny bit of street lights peered through the boards, just enough for me to be able to see the lines on the paper which I poured my heart out in writing. I would write and cry and drink until I fell asleep with the pen in my hands. The waters were my peaceful place. Things I wasn't able to tell anyone I was able to write about and relieve my pain on my own. Writing was always my outlet. It was my escape from reality or my challenges I didn't want to face but yet faced by force. It was my strength. My mother always told me "Anyone can take everything from you, but what's in your mind, no man can ever take"!

My battlefield was my mind. Once I was able to write I was able to conquer and achieve.

It was only a relief while I was at the beach.

Each time I got back home I was the same person I was when I first arrived there. My peace was interrupted by being bitched at for every little things.

I was restless, afraid, alone, and annoyed with any little thing someone said that I didn't like. I ticked for every little thing as well. My personality drastically changed. I did whatever I wanted. I didn't feel the need to listen to anyone. I disappeared when I needed a break and came back when I felt like it. Things only got worse with me. I stole my dads rent money once and I ran away from home. Of course I felt guilty and came back the next day to take my share of yelling. I sold things to have money to hang out. I was changing and I didn't know how to cope anymore. I was a good person and bad things happened to me. I figured if I was a bad person then good things will happen. I didn't know why all the wrong things were happening in my life and I used that lame excuse and continued to destroy my own life, blaming others every opportunity I had.

I blamed, blamed, blamed...

I blamed everything I did wrong it was because this one did this to me or that one did this to me, damn well knowing that I was responsible for my own actions. I just wanted my family together again with my mother here. I just wanted to go back to normal. Whatever normal was. The longer my mother was away, the more I adapted to a reckless lifestyle. I lashed out for her to come back and sure enough she did.

My mother came home after eight long months. She took another risk to come back for me. She made it in time for my sweet sixteenth birthday as she promised. Unfortunately for her, she came home to a destructive, depressed, suicidial teenage daughter, and a broken home. My mother was the strength in the family. She always knew how to fix everything and make us feel better.

I started getting closer to my mother and began expressing what I was going through and how difficult it was for me while she was away. I opened up and let her in my life, my pains, my joys, my fails, and my success. Our bond grew stronger, not just as mother and daughter, but she was my best friend and the sister I never had.

My mother began to coach me, while getting me the help I needed with an AA (Alcohol Abuse) counselor, at Daytop Village, on Merrick Boulevard, located in Queens. My mother began going with me in support, of helping me to get through and past the urges of alcohol. I completed my program in six months with a certificate. The urges went away within the first two months but I continued the program so I can feel like I have accomplished something, without quitting midway. I gained progress and that was more of a motivation for me, to want to accomplish anything I put my mind to.

During the ages of twelve through sixteen, while I was working on and off for a pandit (Hindu priest) named Krishna, inside of an Indian music, movies, and religious store, there was a guy who constantly bothered me to be his girlfriend. I was twelve he was eighteen. Because of what I was going through I denied him each time, year after year. There were times I even chased him away and called him a stalker. It always felt weird and it made me uncomfortable. There were times I went to work and I would have flowers waiting for me. I would take the bus to and from school he would be right there. I was afraid some days and some I felt sorry for him. I ignored him the entire time not until one day…

I opened up and trusted my mother to tell her about him. Her response was shocking to me.

"Let him chase you. You do not chase a man. That is how you will know he loves you or not". My mom advised me.

She began to give me the warning signs and how to know the difference between "come see me and live with me are two different stories". I didn't understand much but I listened anyways. Mother always had these weird sayings I never really understood, but I listened anyways, in hopes of finding out its true definition. She explained that "patience is a virtue" and that if he truly loves you he will not give up easily. My heart melted at those words and advice. This guy name is Derrick.

Derrick, never gave up. One day he came in and started to cry asking me for one last time to give him an opportunity and stated that he loved me.

That was the day he stole my heart. A smile was all it took from me to ease the pain in his heart. I felt better and began to look at him with love rather than fear. Time progressed and each time I got better at lowering my guards and allowing him to freely enter my life. He made my life worth living. I couldn't believe that the same person I was so afraid of could have stole my heart and change my way of thinking. He didn't give up on me and that was the most important thing for me. We started spending more time together and got to know each other even better. After a year of dating we took the next step, in being intimate. Derrick was the first guy I ever gave myself freely to, since the rape. I was confused what to do but he guided me through it and made love to me. I was unable to focus through the entire time because I still cringed at the thoughts of penetration. And this time he was penetrating me, sending chills up and down my spine. My body was doing things I didn't know was capable of. Derrick occupied most of my time after that first night we laid in each others arms. I was emotionally, and sexually attached to him. I told him everything about myself and what happened to me and to my surprise he was there with listening ears never judging me. I was comfortable to talk to him.

After a long while, I began to see changes in Derrick. He started drinking more than usual. I would have to leave my house and meet him at bars and bring him home because he was too drunk and wouldn't leave unless I went to get him. I ended up getting stuck quite a few times at the bar waiting for him to finish his last drink. Eventually, he started offering me to drink with him and I accepted. I didn't realize that I was encouraging his habits by drinking with him and each time I drank he would fight with the men in the bar for even looking in my direction.

Derrick had a lot of jealous issues which I didn't notice right off the start. He never cared much to what I wore or who I spoke to, where I went or what I did when he was sober, but the second he started drinking he would turn into a maniac; not towards me but to anyone who looks at me.

We were invited by Derrick brother Jimmy and his wife Leela for dinner and drinks. We arrived there early to help with preparations, but Leela had it under control. Derrick and his brother was drinking outside in front, while Leela and I were talking in the kitchen. An hour had passed and I went downstairs to check up on them. They were fine. Derrick expressed two me that he has to go to the store and if I needed anything to let him know before he leaves. I didn't need anything. Derrick walked away towards the direction of the store, kissing me before he left.

I began to walk up the stairs leaving his brother downstairs by himself and his brother called out for me to wait. I stopped in my tracks and waited to see what it was that he made me stop for. He began talking as I listened attentively. "Would you let me fuck you" He asked.

"Are you insane"? I responded.

I abruptly walked away with anger and hurt. Jimmy then grabbed me and pushed me against the stairs and started ripping my shirt with his teeth. I started to scream as loud as I could. Jimmy's wife was unable to hear my cries for help because she had the music extremely loud. Derrick, however heard my screams and ran to my rescue. Without hesitation or questioning he ran past his brother on top of me, up the stairs and into the kitchen. I can hear him fumbling through the kitchen draws. There were sounds of metal clinging together. I assumed it was a knife or some sharp object.

Derrick ran back down the stairs as Leela ran behind him to find out what's going on or what Derrick was up to. My head tilted back in search for Derrick. A few moments I saw him running towards me and Jimmy and he pushed Jimmy off of me. I got up as soon as I could and Leela ran to me asking what happened. I was unable to answer her after all that was her husband. While she questioned me Derrick ran out the door after his brother. Jimmy never made it out of the yard because Derrick stopped him with a deep laceration on the left side of his face, from his ear to his mouth. Leela heard Jimmy screams and ran past me to stop Derrick from swinging the knife again, and in the process she received a slash across her right shoulder. Neighbors called the cops during the argument and when Derrick had the knife going towards Jimmy for the second time the cops arrived with guns in hands and told Derrick to drop his weapon. Derrick was arrested and taken down to the 75th precinct. The ambulance took Jimmy to the hospital and Leela assisted at his side. I couldn't bare to see Derrick in handcuffs. I know what he did was wrong, but he was defending me. I ran home hysterical and begged my mother and father for their help to get him out of jail. It was the weekend and Derrick couldn't see the judge until Monday morning the cops stated. It was the hardest two days I had to wait to know what they would do to him. He called me later that night from Central bookings, and I began crying on the phone while he was trying to assure me he will be home soon. I didn't know much about the jail system and I believed him.

Monday morning finally came, and I had to appear in arraignment court to hear the verdict. My hands and feet were cold as ice but sweaty at the same time, although it was 85 degree weather outside. I was so nervous and scared. I heard the court officer speaking

"Honorable judge Linda presiding, courts now in session, remain seated, put away all electronics, there are no videoing or photography allowed in this court room, no eating, no chewing gum, no drinking and no talking".

"Presenting to you Derrick Wayne, Number 16 on the calendar, Docket number 441442443, assault in the first and second degree, attempted murder in the second degree, assault with a deadly weapon, resisting arrest, violation of probation" The court officer read off Derrick's charges and the list continued.

I didn't understand what the degrees were about but I sure understood assault, attempt murder, and deadly weapon. This wasn't looking good at all. I began to panic at this point. The courts took a break for lunch around 12:30pm and resuming at 2:00pm. They took Derrick and placed him behind the doors on the opposite side of the court room. The judge stated they will make a decision wether to set bail or not after their break. I had almost 2 hours of spare time before courts started back.

I decided to go to an older friend of mine job directly opposite of the courts. Her name is Reshma. Reshma was ten years older than me. She had a major influence in my drinking habits but also the main person who always encouraged me to continue my writings. Reshma and I worked for the same place when I was twelve until I was about fourteen years of age. Reshma and I were extremely good friends, when I use to cut school, I would go by her home and we would write poetry together. Reshma would sneak me drinks sometimes and we would go out for lunch once in a while. She would beg my mother to take me out at nights and allowed me to go see Derrick or we would double date. Reshma and Jimmy had taken a liking to each other and it was great for me and Derrick because we got to see each other more when Reshma got me out of the house. Jimmy, ended up cheating on Reshma and Leela at the same time. Reshma was very heartbroken by his betrayal that she just stayed away. When I arrived at Reshma job, after not seeing her almost a whole 8 months, it was like we picked up from where we left off. She was an awesome big sister to me. When she questioned what I was doing in the area and I told her what occurred that Friday evening, she immediately got her things together from the real estate office she was the manager for, and told me she was taking me out for lunch. She notified the front desk she was leaving for the day and to forward all calls to her voicemail.

After our lunch; which we barely touched, we headed over to the courts. There was that feeling inside of me again. That feeling of uncertainty, although I was trying to stay positive, all these thoughts were racing through my mind. It was like a gigantic Rubik'x cube with so many bright colors but being colored blind, unable to fit the correct colors in its order.

Reshma disturbed my thoughts with a wave of her hands in my face, to proceed forward through the metal detectors, to be searched before we can enter the court rooms.

I walked forward as directed by an officer, with my head down and tears in my eyes. I wondered if Derrick ate anything in the past two days, if it was hot or cold in the cells, if he regrets what he did because of me or if his love changed for me. I couldn't stay focus on what I was doing, wether I was going or coming. I just kept thinking.

Finally, we cleared security and we were in the court room. The judge recalled Derrick case. The district attorney presented the case and asked for a new court date as the legal aid attorney fought for bail on Derrick's behalf. The judge called both parties up to the counter where no one else could hear what they were saying. A few moments later they returned to their position away from the judge's counter and then, the judge spoke.

"Bail denied"!

The judge denied his bail, and sent him to Rikers Island until his next court date. The next hearing was three months away. I lost it that moment and blurted out "Why"? "Why does he have to wait so long and why was he denied bail"? I yelled out, not specifically to anyone in particular.

The officers had to escort me out of the court room and told me that I can speak to Derrick's attorney afterwards. I waited for almost thirty minutes and my patience began to grow thin. I reentered the court room and requested that I speak to the attorney immediately. I was then sent back out once again and waited an additional ten minutes. Reshma nor I really spoke during this time because she noticed I was already in fumes and didn't want to say the wrong thing to add fuel to the fire. She sat quietly and waited by my side.

"Ms.Ray, Mr.Wayne was denied bail due to his outrageous behavior. He is a danger to society when he is under any influence of alcohol. In the meantime, you go home and get some rest, as early as next week I will put in a request for bail reconsideration. Until then, here is where he will be going, you can call the number in 24 hours and they will provide you with his housing building number, his visitation days and times and things he is allowed to have in there. This is my card, you can reach me at any method and I will fill you in on the details. Have a good day Ms.Ray". Legal aid Fredrick stated.

Reshma and I walked out of the court house and headed back to her home. We started drinking black label rum and coca cola, chasing it with corona and we ordered chicken wings as our cutters. I went home that night drunk out of my mind and lost for words.

When I got in the house, both my parents asked me how much was Derrick bail. Obviously I couldn't give them the amount because his bail was denied. So I told them he won't be on bail until the next court date which was three months away, if the attorney couldn't get him a bail hearing sooner than that, and I walked away. Straight to the showers and in my bed with the house phone by my side, awaiting Derrick's phone call. I waited up all night for Derrick to call but he didn't. I didn't go to work the next day because I wanted to be home when his call came in. I stayed with the phone practically glued to me the entire day until 6 pm that evening finally I heard his voice.

"Princess (the calling name he gave me), I love you and I miss you. Please get me out of here". He began saying.

"I am trying my best, I promise I will do whatever I can. I will call your mom as soon as I hear something from your lawyer". I said.

"Please come visit me". He asked with a soft and tender voice.

"I will come this Wednesday on your visiting day. I have to ask your mother if she will be going or if she wants to come together with me". I explained.

"Okay, I love you Princess, I have to go". He said.

"I love you too baby". I said as I sniffled.

"Stop crying please. For me please stop". He said.

I heard the dial tone right after he spoke and I was unable to respond. His free six minutes phone call was over.

Wednesday had arrived and Derrick's visiting time was from 2 pm until 8 pm. Each visit lasted only one hour. I called Derrick mother and asked if she would like to go with me. She expressed that she would love to, however before we leave she wanted to pick up some clothing for Derrick to wear inside there. We went shopping for Derrick on Liberty avenue and Eldert lane in Brooklyn at a store called ABC's. We weren't allowed to bring in certain colored clothing so we stood with the basic colors (white, grey, and black).

After shopping, Derrick mother and I walked down about a block away from the store we were at and got on the A train. It was my first time going to a jail to visit anyone. We had to transfer from one train to another then took the bus going over the bridge to the jail. No one was allowed to enter the facility unless authorized. Those who drove to the facility had to park in the parking lot and still take the bus over the bridge. It was a quiet travel between his mother and me. I didn't feel like saying much because I felt like I was the cause and here this woman stands who both her sons were hurt and I wasn't sure how she felt about the situation. I blamed myself entirely. Although none of it was my fault I still felt responsible.

When we arrived at the facility, people started running off of the bus to form a line. I took my time walking. About two hours had passed and we were still on line waiting to enter the building. I didn't realize that was the reason everyone was rushing to join the line.

When we got to the front of the line, the officers were checking for Identifications. I didn't have any ID with me. I didn't know I had to bring any form of ID and so only Derrick mother was allowed in. I sat outside in the 96 degree weather, with the sum beaming on me, for almost five whole extra hours. I paced back and fourth wondering if everything was okay in there. I remained unsettled until Derrick mother finally came back out of the building. The same way we got there was the same we got back. On the ride going back Derrick mother started talking to me.

"I left him a $100 dollars, three outfits, three boxers, three vests and some stamped envelopes so he can always write to you. He started crying before I left and he said to tell you he loves you and he would call as soon as the money reaches his commissary. He said for us to keep calling the attorney". His mother began to explain how the visit went.
"Thank you, ma. I will call as soon as I reach home". I assured her.

When we got home it was about 9:30 pm. I spent the entire day miserable and just wanted my bed at that point. Around

11:30 am the following day, I awoke with such a huge headache. I brushed my teeth, showered and got dressed, drank a cup of lemon and green tea, and got on the phone right after. I continued calling the lawyers office, bail bonds, courts and so on, in search of helping Derrick to getting a bail.

Finally after two days of constant nagging to everyone, I got a phone call from Derrick. We didn't speak since two days prior his visit with his mother until today which was Friday. Derrick called me and asked if I would come see him that all visits are from 7 am until 2 pm on Fridays or his next visit would be Saturday from 7 am until 2 pm. Each week the visiting schedule was switched.

"Yes, baby I will come see you. How are you holding up"? I questioned him.

"It is hard being in here and away from you. Why didn't you walk with ID the last time"?He asked.

"I didn't know I had to have any form of ID to enter the building". I explained.

"Well, make sure you do walk with it if you are coming today or tomorrow". He stated.

"I will". I responded.

This time the conversation lasted for about fifteen minutes, rather than a measly six minutes. But when the phone cut off he was able to call again for an additional six minutes. I had no clue of their phone situation in there. It was great talking with him for a longer period of time as he expressed to me that once he has money in his "books (commissary) he would be able to make more calls through the day, unless they were on lock down and unable to use the phones.

As time went by…

I continued visiting Derrick every week for the next two months. I continued working and putting money on his books and I wrote him letters and poetry at least twice a week. I sent him puzzle books and books which he could read and I made sure every call that came in from him I answered.

The first week in the third month I got a phone call from his attorney that he will be produced in the morning for his bail hearing. I called off of work for that day and made myself available to attend the hearing. Derrick didn't call back for me to tell him the great news that night prior to his hearing so I assumed they were locked down for the night.

At the bail hearing...
"Bail set at $10,000 over $50,000". Judge Schwartz; another judge other than the one who did Derrick's arraignment announced.

I waited for the lawyer to come out and speak with me.
"What does ten thousand over fifty thousand mean?" I asked the lawyer.
"Ten thousand over Fifty thousand means that you either come up with the full amount of ten thousand cash or fifty thousand collateral. You can also reach out to the bails bond and see what they say". Replied the lawyer.

I left the courts in hopes of figuring this mess out. I went home and begged my parents, as well as Derrick parents to help get him out. Derrick mother came with a box of jewelry and gave it to my parents and asked for them to keep it until the case was over in exchanged that they paid the full bail. To my surprise my parents agreed. Later that night Derrick mother and I took the train and headed over to the courts. After waiting for almost an hour, the court officer called us up to the front of the line and asked how he can help us. When we told him we wanted to post bail for Derrick, they stated that we needed to go to the Jail itself because the inmate has been transferred back to the facility.

We walked down about three blocks away from the courts and decided to take the train. At first we were hesitant because we were carrying so much cash on the train where it was always busy, but we had no choice. It was the fastest way to the jail. When we arrived, we waited an additional two hours before we saw an Officer to take the bail. Derrick mother had a lot of paperwork to fill out. The papers required her name, address, job, income, two references, and proof of where the money came from. After she filled out the requirements we were told to wait in the front building. We sat down and waited as told. About an hour went by and a Captain in the jail came over to us to discuss the process.

"Mrs.Wayne, this is going to be a while. Bail was posted, but we have to make sure there aren't any warrants active, no probation or parol hold, or no immigration holds. In the meantime you may go home and await Mr.Wayne release". Stated the Captain.
"Excuse me officer" I interrupted.

"Yes, ma'am" He replied.

"Do you have an average of how long the process? We may have to wait. Mr.Wayne doesn't have money on him to get home".

"Ma'am, it usually takes between two to six hours, very rare it is longer than that. Also, any inmate that is released from any facility will be given a metro card to reach their destination. I will give you a number and you can call to check the status of the inmates release. It will say on the recording after you have listened to all the prompts wether the inmate is still in custody or the inmate has been released". He explained.

"Thank you". I replied.

We left the jail at around 1:30 am and got out of the train station around 3:08 am. On our way walking to the home, I walked past my house to walk Derrick mother home first. She didn't want me walking by myself and I didn't want to leave her to walk alone either. I took the initiative and walked her home.

Around 11:15 am Derrick was ringing my door bell and yelling by my window. I immediately jumped out of my bed and ran to the window praying that this wasn't a dream and he was actually there. Derrick was standing with a rose in his hands in the pouring rain and started screaming "I love you".

I went downstairs to open the door and I started to cry then hugged him so tight, not wanting to let go. He was clean shaved, compared to when I visited him. He had on new clothes, shoes and a hat. Derrick and I couldn't stay away from each other for long periods of time because either him or I would begin crying. We both thanked my parents and continued on with our relationship.

Derrick had several court dates one after another, trying to fight his case. Jimmy had pressed charges and decided to drop it after a while, but because the State picked up the matter it was an even harder battle for Derrick to fight.

The trial day has came and I can feel all eyes on me. Derrick parents along with his brother and sister in law were in the court room on one side as I stood directly across the room from them. I felt like an outsider who caused havoc in a happy family. Although, I know I did nothing wrong and I couldn't control Derrick's rage, I still felt like I am to be blamed.

Derrick was convicted. He received five years of probation with an anger management program, an alcohol abuse program, and counseling. I was extremely happy he didn't get any jail time, and also relieved that he would get some help to control his anger issues, his jealousy, and his alcohol problems.

I began going to each session with Derrick, as one of his biggest supporter. I attended all classes, therapy, group meetings, substance abuse courses, etc... Things were not the greatest but they were getting better.

My older brother Naresh, found out I was dating Derrick and he went after him. When Naresh found him he began beating on Derrick and broke his nose, warning him to stay away from his sister. The reason Naresh was so upset was because one, I was too young to be dating, two, Derrick was much older than me, Three, I didn't finish school, four, he knew Derrick through a friend of his and heard that Derrick is an alcoholic and he is always in and out of jail.

There wasn't anything I could have done to fix this. I was so hurt by my brothers actions even tough I know he only wanted what was best for me. I left the house and went straight to Derricks parents house where Derrick also lived, which was a few blocks away from where I lived. I didn't care at this point what happened to me. I knew I loved Derrick and I wanted to be with him and start my own family.

Derrick, and his parents welcomed me in. I ate dinner and showered and proceeded to the room with Derrick. I was a bit embarrassed to sleep in the room as his parents room were right next to his and I didn't want to seem disrespectful, but they assured me that it was okay.

Later that night, my brother came to look for me to apologize and begged for me to come back home. I forgave him but I refused to go back. That night I spent at Derricks house was the most hurtful night for me. I slept on the floor with him in his room because the bed which he had was too small for the both of us.

The following morning my brother showed up to the front door of Derricks home,. At first I didn't want to open the door but Derrick told me that we should go down together, although I was afraid of another fight occurring, my brother reassured me from the outside he was there to give me something. with a thousand dollars in his hand and told me "If you will be with him, I do not want you living at any in laws house"! My brother demanded and gave Derrick the money in his hand. They shook hands and hugged and forgave each other.

I was relieved that I didn't have to be torn between my loved ones and the man I loved. That day when Derrick went to work he asked his boss if he knew of any apartment for rent and his boss offered to rent him the two bedroom basement for $600 dollars a month. That evening Derrick came home with a smile on his face and told me to get dressed he's taking me to see the basement apartment. I was excited. When we arrived at the apartment, my brother and mother showed up with a truck filled with appliances, bedding, pots, towels, and much more items to fill a home. I was curious to how they knew about the apartment. Of course when Derrick got the news from his boss he went to see my brother and give him the news. I was surprised that my eldest brother and mother was there to support my decisions.

Finally, we moved in that same night. I only had my clothing to pick up from my mothers home so it was easy for me to pack. We moved in with a furnished apartment thanks to my brother and mother. We didn't lack anything. I dropped out of school completely to pick up another job, because I was on my own now. I left the music store and got a full time job at Expo 2000 clothing store, also working part time after work with children. Derrick worked long hours some days, so with him not being around I took up another job at a car dealership.

We enjoyed each others company, with the little time we had with each other. Unfortunately, Derrick drinking was out of control, and his anger grew more and more each day. One night after partying at my uncle house, Derrick came home with me and started arguing because someone told him that I have different men in the neighborhood that I talk to. He automatically believed and continued arguing back and fourth with me. Eventually, it stopped and he fell asleep. That same night I got up off of the bed and went to use the bathroom. When I got back to the room, he was awake and started yelling and questioning me

"Where did you go"? He questioned.

"I went to the bathroom" I explained.

"You're a fucking whore, cheating on me and think I am stupid" He screamed.

"I never cheated on you, what makes you think that, and where are you getting that from? I work one full time job and two part time, I come home and cook, clean, do laundry and satisfy your needs in bed. Now, tell me what the fuck is your problem and where do I even have the time to cheat"? I demanded in hopes of getting answers.

Derrick, plunged towards me, shoved me on the bed, jumps on top of me, and started choking me. I screamed for help, I tried to fight back but he was too strong. Through the ruffling back and fourth, I was able to get out of his grip and I crawled under the bed. I wanted to make a run for the door but the position he was standing, I would have had to push through him to get to the door.

I heard knocking on the upstairs door and my landlord screaming "What's going on down there"?
"Help me, please help me" I cried and screamed.

Derrick dragged my legs from underneath the bed, picked me up off the floor and threw me against the wall. I began to scream louder and louder, and at this point the landlord was trying to break open the doors himself while screaming out he called the cops. Derrick ran out of the room to the kitchen, and I managed to run behind him closing the bedroom doors and locking it. Derrick heard the door shut; he ran back and began to break the door open only this time he had a knife in his hands and started yelling out "I'm going to chop you to pieces, if I have to break this door open, open the fucking door"! He kept banging until he finally broke the door in. He ran behind after me and kicked me in my stomach onto the bed. He had a carving knife in right his hand. I tackled with him to get the knife out of his hands, in the process my left side wrist got sliced. I couldn't feel a thing, but I saw the blood gushing out my wrist and splattering everywhere. I couldn't defend myself any longer and Derrick took advantage of that by putting the knife down and began to punch me with both hands all over my face and body. I couldn't move my arms, I had already lost a lot of blood and although I was in a rage and my body was numb; unable to feel a thing, I had no strength left in me.

I awoke in the Emergency Room, with my parents at my side. I didn't know how I got there and at what point did I lose conscience. I couldn't remember anything. A Doctor came in the room to give me my medications, asking my parents to leave the room for a while as she needed to examine me.

"Doctor, what day is it? How did I get here"? I asked with confusion in my mind.

The Doctor began to tell me.

"Based on the reports, the cops arrived in the nick of time to stop Derrick as he stood over your body with the knife in his hands pointed downwards and close enough to pierce straight through your chest, while you were passed out. Today is Friday. You have been here since last week Saturday and today was the first time you awoke. We kept you on IV and fed you through a feeding tube while you were unresponsive". The Doctor stated.

I couldn't remember anything; everything just went blank. How could Derrick do this to me. I made him chase after me for so many years and when I finally gave him the opportunity of being in a relationship with me, he destroys me. My heart raced at the thought of him holding a knife over me as I was unconscious. I looked up at the monitor to my left and saw the numbers rising. It was a bunch of squiggly lines going up and down, with a little heart to the side of the screen. My chest was hurting even more at this point. I laid and cried myself back to sleep. The Doctors rushed in and started screaming to pass this and pass that. I couldn't hear the words clear but I knew something was once again wrong with me.

Two weeks later...

I was released from the hospital and referred to see a speech therapist to regain my speech. My brains weren't able to process and respond as I use to. I was much slower and very depressed. I couldn't manage to bounce back from this situation as fast as I wanted to. I was already on the verge of committing suicide when I got raped, I finally pulled through and gave in to loving someone. That love almost got me killed. I got on my knees and began to scream and asked God

"Why me, What did I do so wrong to deserve this pain and suffering in life? I was a good child and dedicated to serving you but you destroyed me" I began to question and blame God for the bad things which happened to me. I searched for answers but none was given. I completely lost my faith and sanity. I stayed away from my family after that happened and I lost interest in a lot of things and I didn't want to speak to anyone about my problems.

Derrick continued to reach out to me through phone calls and letters. I denied all of his calls. I received all of his letters in which I read and shredded, because at this point I lost all trust in him. I was afraid of him. Anything he wrote on paper was irrelevant. The damages were done! I accepted the truth; his love was dangerous to me. I just wanted to heal past the hurt and get through it as fast as possible. I knew that Derick and I would never be in a relationship again.

My brothers took me to the old apartment to pack my things so I can go back to living with my parents. It was three weeks after the incident occurred and walking back into my home where I shared with someone I loved so much was extremely painful for me. There were things thrown everywhere, glass broken on the floor, dishes piled up in the sink, the bed turnt over, and the door for the bedroom half way off of its hinges. I couldn't believe that all of this happened that night. My brothers looked at me with disbelief. I lowered my head in shame and continued packing. I separated my things from Derrick's and I asked my brothers to drop it off to Derrick's mother house for him if and when he was released he would have his things he needed. At this point, I shouldn't have cared but the heart I that I had, wouldn't allow me to be vindictive. Besides, his things served no purpose to me; other than bitter sweet memories. I left the apartment with tears in my eyes, and a lot on my mind.

When my brothers brought me home, they helped me up the stairs and they unpacked my belongings; putting them where they belonged. I was unable to work for a while and I couldn't do much around the house. My body was still in a shock and sore from all the beating I endured. I had no friends around to talk to, no one I trusted, of course bedsides my mother, yet; I wasn't able to express my feelings to her. I wasn't in the mood to read or draw and I wanted a way to get my feelings out.

The District attorney called me about a month later and stated that I needed to appear in courts or I will be held in contempt of not complying to be on the witness stand. Derrick took his case to trial, for hurting me. I couldn't believe it at first until I walked in that court room. I explained to the District attorney that I didn't want to continue with this case, I did not call the cops, and I refuse to press charges. She didn't want to hear that, and she began explaining that I lost lost my life and that the 911 tape which they had when the landlord Mr.Ram, called for help. She then stated that the screams were insanely disturbing and being that this isn't what I wanted, this is what will happen by force, because the State picked up the case already.

The hardest thing for me to do was face the man I loved so much in a court room, as the judge gives him his verdict because of the injuries he caused upon me.

I had no choice or I would have been punished for not going in that court room. At least that was what I was told by the District attorney. The trial began, and evidence was brought in by the state against Derrick. I sat and listened attentively. This time I made sure I didn't blank out and I didn't miss anything. I needed to hear that 911 tape for myself. I was worried how my parents would feel when they also heard. My parents were with me every step of the way during the court dates back and fourth.

The screaming was definitely disturbing to me. My mother and father were hysterical. I couldn't believe that I was being attacked by the man I loved so dearly. I didn't care if he had just slapped me but damn it, he wanted my life. When I heard that recording it just gave me more strength to pick my heart up off of the floor and move on with no regrets.

Finally, the verdict day.

"Mr.Wayne, we the people find you guilty based on the evidence which was provided. Guilty on these charges first degree assault, second degree assault, attempt to injure with a deadly weapon, and attempted murder in the third degree. I hereby sentence you to the maximum penalty up to five years imprisonment and the minimum of one year with good behavior and probation. There is a full order of protection for you to stay away from Ms.Ray, that means No form of contact (No emails, no cellphones, no letters, no third party contact, no text messages) You must stay at least 300 ft away from Ms.Ray. That means, if she is walking on one side of the street you have to go to, then you should wait until she presumed and then go, keep the distance of 300 ft apart". Judge Riley read off his charges he was convicted for, while giving him specific instructions to keep away.

Most of Derrick's charges stuck with him. There was no defense for him, because the recording as well as the pictures the Detectives provided which they took when I was in a mini coma in the hospital; there were enough evidence against him. I didn't even know that those pictures existed. A few moments after the judge read the verdict, the court officers who were already standing behind Derrick, took out their chains and handcuffs, and began shackling Derrick's hands and feet. I looked over towards him and I could feel his anger, his disbelief, his pain, his regrets, and his love burning for me burning to ashes. At least that was how I saw his facial expression as he looked down, while the officers tightened the chains on his waist.

Before the officers took him out of the court room, he looked over at me and yelled "Princess, I love you! Please don't leave me".

The tears began to well up in his eyes, when I made eye contact with him. I knew that was the last time I could ever look him in the eyes. I did it to show him that I was afraid; although deep down inside I was shivering at the thought of all the pain he caused, I was not just afraid but sad and hurt. I wanted him to see me strong, but inside it was eating me alive rapidly and all I wanted to do was cry and break down, throw a tantrum and make this feeling disappear. I looked him in the eyes without tears this time. He knew there was no coming back. When he realized I said nothing in return, he got angry. His words were like daggers aiming for my heart. As the officers began taking him through the door, he started cursing and yelling.

"I will kill you!!! If I can't have you, no one will. Do you hear me, do you fucking hear me"?

I turned my back to Derrick and walked away with my parents towards the exit door. Derrick mother, father and brother got up and walked behind us. As my parents and I exited the door, my mother turned back and try to explain to Derrick mother that I was forced to show up or I would have issues with the law. Derrick mother had tears in her eyes and said "I understand".

She began rambling off while sobbing through each sentence.
"It is the alcohol that has him in this situation, if he would only listen to me and stop the drinking". She explained to my mother.

I had no intentions of justifying anything to anyone. Derrick mother sat there and listened to the 911 call just as my parents did and never leaked a tear; not until the verdict was released by the judge, only then she started screaming about her baby boy and became hysterical. What she failed to see is that her baby boy almost killed me, regardless of his addiction or not to alcohol, there is no excuse to his madness nor does that justify the cause to pled insanity. He was sober on this day but yet he managed to yell out that he will kill me if he can't have me. There isn't anything that can justify that, period. That was when I realized that I would never give him another chance to hurt me again. How could he love me so much if he has the urge of destroying me? I couldn't bare to stand and listen to his mother go on and on, blaming the alcohol he was consuming. I walked away without saying a word and left my mother where she stood, listening to her bullshit. My dad and I walked out of the court house and decided to wait in the car for my mother.

I was trying to get my mind clear of all the mishaps which occurred in my life and the only way I knew of was to write it out. So, I started back my writings and began to pour out everything on paper.

The pain I was going through was my only motivation to write. And so I wrote:

Love's Confusion

As time permits and pleasure demands, I sit at my most tranquil moment to type these few lines letting you know that I love you.

We were born by ourselves…We will Die by ourselves…But as we Live…being alone without a companion is not in Gods design…Isolation can be good for a time…But it also a form of cruel punishment…Reach out and hug someone close to you…Tell Them you love them…
For as often as I can I will continue to say that I love you…
If a strong emotion suddenly lights all the candles we carry inside ourselves,
It creates an explosion or brightness that shines far beyond our normal vision and then a splendid tunnel appears,
That shows us the way that we forget when we were born and calls us,
To recover our lost divine origin…
The soul longs to return to the place it came from,
… Leaving the body lifeless…
And ever has it been that love knows not its own depth until the hour of separation

that you are my oxygen that ignites this fire within me…
I hope that this never be you but always be me and one day our love will blossom and together we will be on the same page.

Unconditional love, hard to find as equality among races
My love, everlasting, forever, understanding and compromising
His love, sudden as a light but strong as the darkness
But as sudden as it can be turned on, sudden it can turn off
Keeping love, strategy is the key
My love, is powerful no matter what, devours the obstacles rain or shine
His love, quickly distracted by newness and temptation of the unknown
Our Love, our mutual agreement
My love says Be mine forever, don't change inside
His love says While you're mine, don't change outside
When time fools you into a false sense of security
My love says, we have history baby, dedication and commitment
His love says, I don't feel the same anymore, we don't have passion
But passion lost was interest lost only to further distance….
Let's try again? We deserve a second chance
My love, excited, refreshed, hopeful; better to try and fail than fail to try
His love, unable to put the best foot forward, can't wait till the motions are over

Unconditional love, hard to find as equality among races.
My love and his love stuck on the same chapter but never on
the same page...

After four long boring and depressing months of being stuck in the house, I finally pulled my mental frame of mind together and began seeking for work. I sent out resumes for all kinds of jobs. Two weeks later and eighty six resumes, I finally got a phone call for an interview, working with children.

I had a lot of experience with children because of my niece and nephew. My eldest brother and his wife had their first child (a boy) Michael when I was at the age of eleven. I knew how to change a baby's pampers, feed them, shower them and clothed them, by age of eleven because my mother was the babysitter when my brother or his wife went to work. I use to watch my mom and always offered my help, eventually I was a professional at taking care of kids. Before I got raped, I spent most of my time going to school, but on my down time I would be with my mother helping her in the kitchen, doing laundry, cleaning the house or taking care of baby Michael. I was ready to accept the job if I was offered it and I was excited.

I got to the interview fifteen minutes before the appointment time. Suzette, a dark skinned tone, 6"ft 2" inches, weighing approximately 250 pounds, wobbled through the door, asking "Who is Summer Ray"?

"It's Samaya Ray, that's me". I answered.

"Come in please".

I approached Ms.Suzette with a smile, because I've learnt that first expression says a lot about someones character. I didn't want to seem depressed or angry at the world, although I was. I just needed a job that I would love to do, to take my mind off of things. I kept eye contact, straight up right body posture, hands clasped in front of me like a lady, with my legs crossed one over the other, through the entire interview with Ms.Suzette. She never took her eyes off of my paperwork to even notice that I did everything right. She was I shock at my report card. For someone like me that began cutting school almost the entire semester, I had excellent scores. I was an A plus in school minus the attendance. The initial interview was to take care of children, but she changed it to just tutoring.

"Ms.Ray, you have extremely well grades and I would like to know if you would be able to tutor as well as mentor six children (ages 11-17) at the same time. The pay will be $20.00 an hour, four hours a day, five days out of the week starting at 3 o'clock pm until 7 o'clock pm". Ms.Suzette explained.

"Yes, I would love that". I replied.

"Okay great, see you starting next week Monday at 2 o'clock pm. Welcome to the institution for children with special needs". Said Ms.Suzette.

"Thank you". I said.

I began working with children who had ADHD (Attention, Deficit, Hyperactivity, Disorder).
My job was easy and I enjoyed every moment of it. Although, I was heart broken and depressed those children gave me a reason to look forward to waking up each morning. The children were very loving and full of energy. As time went on I began to teach the kids how to use their hands as a tool to create

things. I gave them science projects, puzzles, building with popsicle sticks, and much more interesting and hands on activity. They absolutely adored me, and I couldn't get enough of their cheerful spirits.

A year later Derrick was released....

One day I was walking towards the A train station, located on Grant Avenue in Brooklyn, and I barely spotted someone who looked like Derrick. At first I wasn't sure, but I hid behind a black pickup truck to take a peak. It was him after all. I was afraid after all he did to me. The trust was completely destroyed and although I loved him so much, I knew it was a dangerous relationship. I lowered my head and carried on towards the train station. Either way, if I went back towards my home he would see me, but I chose to continue my journey to the train. I didn't think he would be so daring or bold enough to hit me in public where there would be witnesses.

I was wrong...

Derrick yelled out for me and I pretended to not hear. I kept walking faster as I began to hear foot steps behind me. I wasn't sure if it was him or not because I was too afraid to turn back and face him.

"Bitch, I am calling you! Are you deaf"? He continued

I briskly walked into the train station and asked the MTA attendant to please call the cops. She began with a million and one questions before she decided to call, but it was too late. Derrick, came in right behind me and grabbed me by the hair, began dragged me out of the station while screaming what a whore I was; I neglected him and I caused him to go to jail. I tried to plea my cause and explain I was forced to be there, but he was not trying to comprehend that. He was stuck on his anger and the rage he had which bottled up inside for the entire year in which he claimed I neglected him. I thought for sure he would kill me this time around. He had such a tight grip on my hair as he dragged me through the two way streets of oncoming traffic.

"Please, please stop! I'm begging you". I begged and pleaded with my hands wrapped around his legs, as my buttocks grazed against the concrete roads.

Derrick picked me up off of the ground and braced me against a store front gate with his left hand wrapped around my neck, while his right hand held a knife to my stomach, and I had both of my hands around his forearm trying to release the grip he had around my neck. I was petrified. By standers watched on, as I screamed for help. Finally, the owner of the Dominican deli in which Derrick braced me against their side gate, came out and told Derrick, he has called the police. Derrick didn't listen right away after the man had spoken. He just continued to choke me, until his father was walking past to go to the train, for work and saw and intervened.

The relationship between Derrick's father and I was great. His father always stood up for me and gave me the most utmost respect. Likewise, I also had much love, and respect for the man. Thankfully, I was able to breathe after Derrick released his hands when his father commanded him to. I could smell the liquor on Derrick breath and it was only 8:30 am. I figured he drank all night into the morning and just waited around for me to walk pass. The love which I had for Derrick, began growing into hate. I never imagined a day that I would ever feel that way about him. He caused me a lot of pain, which distracted me from the rape and constantly feeling sorry for myself.

I went back home that morning, unable to go to work because my throat was sore, I was in a shock and I was afraid. I didn't want to tell my family because, I was afraid my brothers or father being locked up and sent away. Each day became harder for me to walk through the streets. First the rape, then the man who claims to love me has been abusing me, and I wonder what's next. I began to lose hope and trust in people.

Derrick saw me several times going to or from work, grocery stores, or waiting at the bus stop or train station and each time the abuse got worse. I began having nightmares after each time he would go into attack mode.

One day, Derrick caught me coming out the doorway of my house to go towards the train station, and he said he just wanted to talk so he, followed me until I was at the corner of the block and started arguing with me. I kept walking away because I knew eventually it would become physical, and he grew more angry. An hispanic middle aged woman, was coming out of the coffee shop the same time I was crossing the streets and she looked over and saw the way Derrick grabbed me and kept tugging at my arms back and fourth yelling and spitting.

"Leave her alone"! She yelled.

"Mind your fucking business, bitch"! Derrick screamed back in anger.

The woman got on the phone and called 911. Derrick heard her on the phone and he finally let go of my arms and told me to stay right there. From the moment he let go of my arms and crossed over the street the woman told me to run. But I couldn't move much because my entire body was aching, so I tried to walk as fast as I could when his back was turnt. The woman walked with me, almost two blocks away to a much busy area on Liberty Avenue and Forbell street. The woman told me to wait right there and used her passcode to unlock the bank door. She worked in Washington Mutual Bank directly where we were standing awaiting for the police to arrive.

I began to feel sorry for Derrick, but I couldn't take the abuse anymore. Anything that would keep him away at this point would help. Unexpectedly, Derrick got close enough to throw a Heineken beer bottle in my direction, hitting me on the left side of my forehead and cutting me. He then yelled out,

"I told you I will give you something to call the cops about"! Yelled Derrick.

The woman ran out the door and to my rescue. There was so much blood leaking from my head and covering my eyes, she began to wipe away the blood from my eyes, with her bare hands. I was shocked that she didn't scorn my blood, and ever so grateful for the way she tried to protect and care for me. A total random stranger has showed me love and care after all.

Derrick fled the scene before the cops and ambulance arrived. The cops started questioning me about my name, date of birth as well as, Derrick's name and date of birth. I gave them whatever information they needed. At this point I didn't care about being called a snitch in the streets because I was fed up. I was fed up of always being broken, mentally and physically. I didn't care what happened to Derrick any longer. The cops took the information I gave together with the description the woman gave as well as her written statement and contact information, then proceeded back to their car and began looking up Derrick information. At that point the paramedics took me in the ambulance and began cleaning me up.

The officers returned to the ambulance and showed me a picture of Derrick and asked if it was him. I nodded my head up and down, showing signs of yes, at the mugshot picture from his last arrest. The officers began telling me that there was a full order of protection in effect and Derrick will be charged and convicted the maximum penalty for violating the order.

"What is the maximum penalty"? I questioned.

"The minimum is one year, with good behavior in jail and the remaining four years of probation, the maximum is five if he doesn't have good behavior or refuses to comply with authorities, however; he will also have additional charges for harassment and assault with a weapon". The officer replied and began to walk away towards his vehicle.

"Okay. Excuse me officer, would you be able to give me the woman name and phone number so I can thank her for being there for me"? I questioned.

"Unfortunately Ma'am, we are not allowed to disclose any information of any witnesses due to their safety"! The officer explained.

The Paramedics interrupted to notify the officers that I needed stitches, and they had to rush me to the hospital.

I was then taken to Brookdale hospital, located in Brooklyn, NY for treatment. I received 26 stitches on my forehead, a neck brace, prescribed Ibuprofen for the pain, and was discharged a few hours later that day.

I wasn't able to speak to anyone when the cops arrived so I was never granted the opportunity to thank the lovely woman who helped me. I didn't have any contact information for her and the officers weren't allowed to disclose information about witnesses. But I promised to never forget her face, so that one day I may see her and personally thank her.

I walked in the house not speaking to anyone in my home, angry, bitter and hurt. Everyone knew by now to not ask me anything, because they were not getting a reply, so they left me alone and I went through it all (emotionally and physically) by myself. My writing is what kept me sane.

I kept in contact with the detectives to find out if they ever caught Derrick. Unfortunately, for me they didn't. I stayed in my home writing my life away, unable to go outside for anything because of the fear in which Derrick put in me.

Cruel love

Alas, cruel love, away with you!
Attempts at you are but in vain!
You tempt and mock at every turn
And always leave my heart in pain.
My thoughts of you must not be real,
A fantasy to never be found.
If this be true, then set me free
That my deep sorrows may be drowned.
Away with your false promises
Of undying, deep devotion
And forever love, if such exists,
I'm done with this emotion!

For there's no hope for such a fool
Whose pleas remain unrequited
For life has left my broken heart
Scarred and forever blighted.

Love Knows

Not it's powers until the time of separation

A few months later...

I received a phone call, from the Sheriff department out in Tampa Florida.

"Princess, it's me". Derrick, said.
His voice made me so angry, I began yelling.

"Why are you fucking calling here"? I questioned.

I knew he was in the system and I was safe, so I took advantage of speaking my mind. I wanted him to hear everything I had to say while he was sober, so he could think of all the damages he caused upon me.

Not giving him a chance to reply to my question, I continued rambling off…

"What you did to me was unacceptable, hurtful, and disrespectful. I trusted you, but you betrayed me. I believed in you, but you lied to me. I thought you was worthy of the love I gave you, but you destroyed it. Why, do you insist in popping up whenever you feel like to cause me emotional or physical harm. Haven't you done enough damages? You are a liar, and I was the fool to believe you. I was wrong to believe you would protect me, and love me unconditionally and accept me for who I am, and what I've been through at a young age. I can't believe that I let my guards down, confided in you, and in return you diminished the little light of hope I had left in me; believing that your love was true. You broke the trust I gave you. You replaced my pain and love for you; with anger and hate. What more do you want to do to me that you haven't done already? Enough is enough and I am fed up of running, hiding, and getting hurt. You have always had my support with your job, your family, your classes, and your incarcerations. I left my parents home and tried to make a life with you, but you ruined that. You ruined me. You physically and emotionally abused me, humiliated me and disgraced me, in public and behind closed doors. What more can you possibly do other than kill me? Please stop chasing after me! I am begging you, please stop! You need to stay the fuck away from me and my family! There will be severe consequences if you ever try to hurt me again. This time I promise I will KILL YOU, THEN YOUR ENTIRE GENERATION AFTERWARDS! And I don't care what happens to me. I refuse to take your abuse any longer. Do you understand me"? I questioned.

There was a long pause between my question and his answer.

"I am sorry, please forgive me". He said.

I immediately hung up the phone after he spoke the words which I cared less to hear.

Finally, it was over! I felt so relief that I got everything off of my mind, without worrying of being attacked.

The District Attorney who was handling the case against Derrick in NY reached out to me a few minutes after I spoke to Derrick, to notify me that he was caught in Florida for driving under the influence of alcohol and without a license. The District attorney then explained that Derrick will be charged with the assault, causing physical injuries with a weapon and fleeing from the scene, also that the order of protection remains in effect.

"Ms.Ray, allow me to explain Mr.Wayne's convictions in further details, and you may ask me any questions afterwards". The District attorney said.

"Sure, I am listening". I replied.

"Mr.Wayne was charged with, violation of a full order of protection against you, fugitive from NYS (New York State) jurisdictions, DUI (Driving under the influence), Assault in the first, second and third degree, Attempted murder in the first degree for the laceration on your forehead, and Assault with a weapon. Do you have any questions for me?". She stated and then asked.

"No, No, thank you. Have a great day". I answered.

"You too, Ms.Ray".

I carried on with my life knowing that I was safe as long as Derrick was behind bars. I hate to look at it that way, but Derrick had already caused enough damages. I knew if I could get through the rape, I would get through and past this bullshit.

Silence your agony

Silence your Agony
Treasure the painful, and beautiful memories
Embrace the journey
Inhale, exhale
Escape
Silence your agony
Remove your pain
Replace it with a passion
Elevate your mind
Learn new traits
Be silent and listen attentively
Silence your agony
Remove acrimony
Replace it with euphony
Dedicate time and stay focused
Life is worth it
Get motivated
Improve your capabilities
As time passes by
Slowly your agony will be diminished

Chapter 3
A New Love....

Two years later...

I finally got my drivers permit and was excited to drive. The day that I got my license, my baby brother Amit and my parents went to pick out a vehicle for me at the Toyota car dealership in Queens. My brother surprised me that day with a brand new 2004 Toyota Corolla sports edition, a year fully paid insurance, and a week of driving lessons.

One week later my brother handed me the keys upon completing my driving lessons. I was so excited, I began jumping for joy, hugging and kissing my brother and parents. I promised that I would get a job and maintain the vehicle and so I did.

Avinash, a guy who lived a few houses from where I lived on Lincoln Avenue, approached me one day and asked
"How have you been"?

Avinash was a family friend of Derrick's family. At first I hesitated in answering but I eventually broke down and told him how I was so hurt. I began telling him all the crazy things that Derrick did to me. Although I was skeptical at first, I had to let anyone who inquired know that I was completely innocent and that Derrick were the cause of his own troubles.

"I am slowly healing from the emotional and physical pain" I responded.

"That's good to hear" Avinash replied.

"Hey, by chance do you know anywhere hiring even if it is a part time"? I questioned.

"Yes, my job is hiring. I can take you tomorrow to meet the boss in person if you like". Avinash answered.

"Sure, I would appreciate that. What time do you want us to meet up"? I asked.

"I have to be at work for 9 am, I usually leave around 7:30 am by train. How would you get there?" He asked.

"I will be driving there, if you want you can get a ride with me". I stated.

"Sure thing. I would appreciate that. See you around 7:30 am". He said.

That morning Avinash came to my house and we headed to his job site. On our way, we ended up hitting traffic on the Southern State Parkway, so we had some time to chit chat. Avinash, assured me that the job would not be difficult for me to handle and he would also be there to show me what to do. We got to the job and Avinash introduced me to the Boss. It was a very short and simple interview. The Boss began explaining the hours and pay, then questioned if I agree to accept the job.

I did!

Each day for almost three weeks, Avinash and I went to and from work together in my vehicle. We had an opportunity to become good friends.

One day I got a much better offer from all the resumes I sent out, working in the sales department for the car dealership called World Trade Auto Sales, and so I decided to leave the job which Avinash helped me to get, taking the offer immediately. I didn't know how to tell Avinash I was sorry for such short notice and for the embarrassment I may have caused him, knowing that he pleaded to his boss to give me the job in the first place, but I had no choice and I built up the courage and eventually told him.

That evening, I picked up my last pay check, shook hands with the Boss, apologized for the short notice and thanked him for the job. I explained to him that I needed something closer to my home as well as the pay was much more, and I got a full time schedule, also flat salary and commission for each vehicle I sell. Mr.Ravi, wished me luck with a smirk on his face. I could tell from the facial expression he was not happy at all.

Later that evening...

"Hey, we have to go out to celebrate your great news" Avinash stated.

"I'm not really up to doing anything" I replied.

"You should, it would be fun and you never know you might meet someone nice. You need to get out of that funk and give yourself a break and enjoy life to its fullest". Avinash said trying his best to convince me.

Avinash continued to plead his cause of us going to hang out. At first I was indecisive, but somehow he managed to convince me. I owed him that much for getting me the job when I needed it.

"Fine, damn it. Fine! You got it. Now stop whining! So what time should I be ready"? I questioned.

"8-8:30 Pm is okay for you"? He asked.

"Yes, that's fine". I answered.

"Okay, see you later". He said with a smile.

"Okay, later". I responded.

I was dressed by 8:30 Pm. I wore a blue and white spaghetti strap shirt, with a short above the knees flared out skirt, 6 inch open toe shoes with my hair down to my waist in tiny curls. I had on silver chandelier earrings with a silver neck choker, and a silver clutch.

Avinash and I met up at around 8:38 Pm that night in front of my house.
"You look amazing". Avinash said.

"Thank you, I tried". I replied with a wink in one eye.

I was legal to enter the bar but not legal to purchase alcohol or drink. I didn't understand why I was going in the first place but oh, well.

When we arrived at the bar it was a few blocks away from the location where I was raped, and so my mind was already on it's own verge of destruction. I wished I could bump into that disgusting animal while I was there. We walked right in, no questions asked by anyone of the staffs nor were there any bouncers asking for identification.

Avinash walked in front of me and pulled out a chair "have a seat, what would you like to drink"?He questioned.

"I am sorry but I don't accept drinks from anyone. It's just my thing since I was twelve years old. Please don't feel bad". I explained.

"Sure, no problem. I totally understand". Avinash said.

"How about I buy you a drink"? I asked.

"If you insist, but next round is on me, and you can have the bar tender make your drink in front of you. If that is okay with you of course". He replied.

"Fair enough". I answered.

"What are you having tonight young woman"?Asked the female behind the counter.

"May I have, an Apple Martini, and whatever he is having add to my bill as well please and thank you". I answered.

"I will be right back with your drinks". She stated.

"Excuse me ma'am". I called out.

"Yes, you can call me Julia". She answered.

"My apologies, Jessica would you possibly be able to make my drink in front of me"? I questioned.

"Why, yes of course I can". Jessica replied.

"Hey, I don't mean to leave you by yourself for a few but I want to go have a smoke. If you want you can come have one with me until she is ready to make your drink". Avinash said.

"Wait, I will go with you. I don't know anyone here and I don't want to be by myself". I replied.

We went outside for a few minutes had our smoke and went right back in.

I noticed that a guy was sitting to the left side of where I was sitting by himself. He waved over to Avinash to get his attention and so Avinash walked over to say what's up to him.

"Hey, what's up bro? Long time no see. Who's the beauty with you"? The guy asked. I over heard their conversation bits and pieces.

"She is my friend, more like a sister to me. Ill introduce you to her". Avinash said.

I was nervous to even talk to anyone after what I went through. Julia brought the empty glass over to me and made the drink in front of me. The guy Avinash was talking to reaches over and pays before I could ask how much.
I looked him straight in the face, with such anger in me.

"Who are you, and why did you do that"? I questioned angrily.

"Hi beautiful, My name is Rajin. I apologize for being rude". The guy replied.

"Thanks but no thanks". I answered.

"May I know your name"? Rajin asked.

"Samaya, my name is Samaya. Nice to meet you. Have a goodnight". I responded in a sarcastic way and a heavy tone of voice.

"Have a goodnight? Sweetheart the night has just began". Rajin said.

"Avinash, please come get your friend before I go in his throat with my heels". I looked over and yelled to Avinash.
"Bro, let us go outside and talk". Avinash said to Rajin.

I finished my drink and decided to use the time they were outside to go to the restroom.

"Bro, she is hard to get. Trust me she's a very beautiful person inside and out but she's not easy as you think. Don't let the way she drinks or the way she is dressed fool you. She has a good head on her shoulders and she has been through a very difficult time. She is now healing after her ex abused her". Avinash said , trying to turn Rajin mind against not talking to me.

"Yo, Avi I will get that. Trust that bro. She already in the palm of my hands". Rajin stated.

"Yea okay, if you say so". Said Avinash.

"Aiight, place your bet nigga". Rajin said to Avinash.

"I'm not betting anything. She already made it clear she cares about me like a brother. Obviously, I am going to lose, duh". Avinash replied.

"Okay, so bet me I can't get her number". Rajin said.

"Bet, you can't and won't". Avinash said.
They came back inside and sat down next to me.

"Would you like another drink sweetheart"? Asked Julia.

"Yes, what else can you make that isn't so sweet but not too bitter either"? I asked.

"You can try a Cosmopolitan. It is pretty good. Most females order that or an Amaretto sour.". Julia said.

"I'll try the Cosmopolitan". I answered.

"Great choice, I will be right back". Julia said.

Rajin, approached me again with a huge koolaid smile on his face.

"So, sweetheart, how old are you"? Rajin asked.

"Again, with you". I replied.

"Yes, again with me. I won't stop bothering you until I get that number of yours".

"What do you want with my number, sir"?

"I want to take you out for a nice candle light dinner, or something sometime, and get to know you more". He explained.

"Look, I am not ready to get to know anyone right now. I am now getting my life back together and I don't mean to be rude, but men aren't on my priority list at the moment. If it's anything, they are on my shit list and I have no trust in any". I said.

"Well, how can you start trusting anyone if you don't give yourself a chance to get to know someone"? He asked.

He did have a point. I kind of liked his personality, his smile, his outfit, his blunt persistence, and the way he licked and bite his lips, and made eye contact when he spoke to me. There was definitely something in him that made me want to give him the opportunity to get to know me. He had some swag in him.

Avinash, was busy trying to get the bar tender phone number who was serving us while Rajin was trying to talk his way into me giving him my number. Julia, came over with another round for us and asking wether I wanted to switch my drink of choice or if I wanted the same as the last one. I chose the Amaretto sour this time while Rajin and Avinash had Hennessy with coke.
"So will you grant me that chance sugar bowl"? Rajin asked.

"718-555-5555" I said and smiled.

"Is that a blush I see"? Rajin asked.

"Maybe, maybe not". I giggled.

Yes, he had me blushing. He had me curious. He had my undivided attention and I had his.

I looked at the time on my Nextel phone and It was already 2:00 Am. The night was coming to an end. I had to be home by 12 midnight and I knew I would definitely hear it from my parents for coming home at that hour.

"It was nice meeting you, you have my number give me a call sometime, but I have to go". I stated as I retrieved my bag and presumed to get Avinash.

"Can I have a hug from you before you leave"? Rajin asked.

"Sure" I answered.

He got up and gave me a hug. While hugging me his lips barely touched my neck. When he pulled away, I turned my face the same time accidentally my lips touched the sides of his lips. I was shy, so I lowered my head and apologized.

"No need to apologize, maybe one day we will get to that stage". He said.

"Yes, maybe". I said, while clearing my throat.

I signaled for Avinash that I was going to meet him in the car, and I headed out the door.
Rajin stopped me in my tracks.

"Beautiful, would you like some company while you wait on Avi". Rajin asked.

"Yes, sure". I answered.

We began talking, while we walked three blocks away towards my car.

"May I hold your hands". He asked.

"What for"? I questioned with a smirk on my face.

"No particular reason. Just wanted to feel your energy through your touch". He stated.

I reached out my hands and he held on putting me on the inside of the street as he walked on the outer corner.

"Why did you move me from walking on that side of the sidewalk"? I asked curiously.

"Because, from today you're going to be my lady and my lady cannot walk on the outside because that means she is available, but on the inside it means she is taken"! He said.

"Oh, really. That's what you think Mr." I said jokingly. "It's not what I think. It's what I know". He replied.

When we arrived at the car, I unlocked the doors with the remote, I reached over to pull the handle and Rajin stopped me in my tracks "wait, please step aside". He said.
I did, while looking at him awkwardly.

He then opened the car door for me, held my hands and helped me in to sit in the driver seat.

"Thank you". I said.

"You're very welcome, sweetheart". He replied.
He leaned over to kiss me and I pulled away.

"Sorry, I do not kiss first time meeting someone". I stated.

"That's fine, I am sorry". He replied.

Avinash came to the car at that awkward moment, and Rajin and I said our goodnights with a light hug. On the drive home, my eyes were burning so badly, they were practically shutting; I just wanted my bed at this point. I started to talk to keep myself awake.

" Avinash, thank you for convincing me to go out".

"You are welcome, you deserve to be happy".
"Have a goodnight". I said.

"Goodnight" Avinash replied.

I dropped Avinash home and I found parking a few houses away from him so I decided to park and walk down to my house. When I got inside, my mother was awake waiting for me on the inside staircase, with her hands on her hips. I knew she was extremely upset from her facial expression.

"Is this the time you come home? I give you an inch and you take a yard"! My mother said angrily.

"i am sorry, it won't happen again". I replied.

"It better not".

I walked away in silence with my head tilted downwards because I knew I messed up big time by staying out so late; when I was specifically told to be home by midnight.

The following morning I received a phone call from Rajin.

"Good morning, sweetheart". Rajin said.

"Good morning" I replied.
"Do I have the pleasure of taking you out for breakfast"? He asked.

"Ugh, I have such a hangover and my mom is bitching about me staying out so late last night. Maybe some other time". I answered.

"Aw, I am sorry if you got into trouble because of me".

"No, I didn't get into trouble because of you. I chose to stay out".

"Okay, well if you change your mind, or you can escape let me know".
I chuckled.

"Yes, will do".

"Have a great day beautiful lady".

"You too".

After I hung up the phone, I proceeded to clean up the whole house, and cooked. I was rushing to get as much as I could done so I would be able to get out of the house again without getting into trouble. My mom felt sorry for the way she spoke to me and decided to let me go out for a few.

I called Rajin back and we decided to meet up for a late lunch. We laughed and talked so much until my stomach began to hurt. Every day since that day, we spent together. And as time progressed, I became more in-tuned with his charming ways, and romantic gestures. I began to get carried away.

After two years of being in denial that I was being used and abused by Rajin lies I started becoming more and more afraid of his anger. What I thought was love turned into bitter hate. When I began confronting him about things he was doing, he would literally grab me by the throat and pin me against the walls and screamed and spit in my face. He cheated on me several times but with that came lots of physical pains. Rajin mother "Babes" was her calling name. She would pretend she liked me but then get me to do chores around the house and after I was done she would ridicule me and compare me to other past relationships her son had. She stole from me and my family when I brought her to meet my parents the first time. She used my parents credit cards and splurged on things for her and her son. When confronted she denied them of course. However each time a situation occurred and I did go over to clean her home I would find candles with pictures and names of Rajins ex girlfriend and his underneath red candles and my name with a ripped picture of his and his name and mine underneath a black candle. I knew at that moment I was not just in a war with a man and woman but rather I was in a spiritual war fare between knowing something was wrong but yet sticking around just to see how the results are reveled. I was young and naive and already hurt about the past and I tried to fix whatever I thought needed fixing but in the process I lost sight of my life as a woman. I lost hope and I settled for less.

Thats what it was...

I settled for less...

Coming soon
Part 2....

Love Entwined

Love Entwined

Your love
Your love has captivated my inner being
Tangled me into mind blowing sensations
Whirl winds and thunderstorms
Lightening and rain
The loyalty is gained
Respect given with questions asked
No demands made
No boundaries
For this love is stronger than the solar system
Your love has erupted in the depths of my heart causing my soul
to intake all of its chemicals
Burning desires
Though miles apart
Your love leaves me weak
Your love deeper than the oceans
Stronger than Concrete
There's no reason for us to be discreet
I prefer the world to see
Endless blessings flowing through my veins
A remarkable feeling no one will understand
Unless of course
You're heart has felt what I was dealt
A Euphoric taste
Your love held my soul

Create in me

Create in me
A garden of love
Rose petals and
sunflowers
Bright reds and
yellows
Purples and blues
Classical tunes
Create in me a
sanctuary
A place where the
universe respects
me
Where magic happens and love blooms
Create in me
A mystery
For eyes that seeks and a soul that yearns
In hopes of faith and magic
A garden of love
Create in me
A beautiful womb
Bringing fourth life and a peaceful home
Placing good intentions in whatever you do
Create in me
A garden filled with colors of life
Guiding and protecting me with all of your might
Create in me that burning desire
When the body tingles and toes curl
Luring me in and letting me lose control
Create in me
A haven to lay my head
Desiring for love and respect
Create in me
A garden of colors and love

The drug that destroyed her home

His friends, fantasies, alcohol and cocaine
A love so rare
Nothing else matters when two souls connects and becomes one
No one else means much other than their love
When honesty and pleasure becomes hate and regrets
When joy becomes Grey and pain has been dealt
She sat and wondered to herself
All along
Everyone was right
And through it all she was blind
A love so rare
He was thirty she was forty one
He wanted to party she wanted a home
He enjoyed the company of his friends and she spent most of her
time alone
As time went by
The love began to slowly diminish
Snatching all away from what she has built
The grief to leave behind her home
The pain she felt when she made up her mind
She did it with a cleared and conscience mind
Letting love slip away

Through her finger tips they go
Her heart she picks up from the floor
He wanted excitement outside of those walls
She wanted a baby and a garden of love
He destroyed her pride with his disgusted words
His sentences were like daggers to her soul
She lifted her head and motivated herself
Moving forward from the bitter memories which they had
She moved forward with one step after another
Taking back her powerful character
As journey takes her through
She will be okay
Because she is stronger than she seems
And her tears will flow
Many nights without him
But no matter how hard it may seem
She will glisten like the stars at night
With her head held high
Because she has overcome
She has finally stand up for what's right for once
And she's proud of the woman she became
She has higher goals and is worthy of so much more
I pray you're safe now

Am I just a simple being? No, I am not

Am I just a simple being?
No, I am not
I am me
Uniquely formed with the intelligence of a scientist, the strength of a warrior, the love of a mother, the warmth of a friend, the joy after pain, the sunshine after rain, the beauty in the dark, the star that lights the skies, I am uniquely formed a woman of Gods creation.
Am I just a simple being?
No, I am not
I am the prize at the bottom of the cereal box, the toy in the happy meal, the laughter of a clown, the frown upside down, I am the reason for someone else life. I am me
Uniquely qualified!
Am I just a simple being?
No, I am not
I am the Diamond in the rough, been broken and fixed, I've been burnt and yet I healed. I am the sparkle in your fears, I write unity and advice, I live on the edge of life. I've been bruised and disrespected, still I manage to lift my head.
I am uniquely blessed
Am I just a simple being?
No, I am not!
I am the shadow that follows your path, behind your every step of the way. I pray for lost souls and hope that I get found. I am impossible but still I fear, I am human and I make mistakes!
I learn from them in my own way!
I am uniquely Born again.
Am I just a simple being?
No, I am not
I am just me

<u>Please don't take my kindness for weakness</u>

Please don't take my kindness for weakness
I am too strong
I will let you go
I will wipe those tears and brush my shoulders off
Don't ever think for once that I am desperate
I refuse to be anyone's object
I am a woman
In flesh and bones
I stand strong while holding my own
I refuse to be an opinion
And option or a toy
I am a woman who holds on strong to the love and care for
others
I put many people and tasks before myself and
If you asked me to give up something for your love and only
yours
I would rather leave you in the dust wondering where you went
wrong!
So please understand that although you see me crumbling
inside

Don't dare to challenge
my mental state of mind
Because I will walk and never to return
I am bold and brave because I am a strong Woman!

Speaking healing into existence

My healing process,

Today, I have healed! I have healed pass the agony and betrayal of those who have claimed their love for me, healed pass the broken bones and silent shadows of disgust and misery. I have over came before and I am cover coming as I am writing. Writing is my outlet of healing and it will be the reason for my success. I can feel it beating in my throat the joy that is awaiting to explode. I feel free because I have learned and I have conquered releasing the pain, the sadness, and the stress. I have faith that is as little as a mustard seed that things will get better for me and as time progressed I begin to see positive changes around me. I've began to open up more and come out of my shadows of blaming myself and realizing that what has been done should have been forgiven to move forward and self heal. I've learned to become one with my mind and soul. I've learned to appreciate and love me first, before I can give love to others. In doing this, I have accomplished! I have conquered my fears of rejection and accepted that whether or not I am perfection in anyone's eyes it doesn't truly matter, because I love me and once I pour into me everything will flow with Gods grace if it was meant to be. I have battled storms and given up but through it I somehow always managed to pull myself up and face the battle straight on. I've managed to stop running away from problems and challenge it at that moment, letting it not carry through for the next day, holding no grudges and having no regrets and so with faith I continued to pray. I believed that God would help me find a way to get through the tough moments and so I saw it, I felt it, and I experienced it, that was a way of showing me to stand my own and be true to my word. I've paved paths and gotten side tracked yet, I have managed to restore what has been lost.

I carried hate for so long and I had to release my negative energy, so I found ways to learn to love again and revive my soul from the enemy. I didn't love myself and so looking in the mirror was scary, not until I found my peace and tranquillity was I able to embrace life's beauty. I had anger built up inside, draining my mind and filling up my soul with resentment against love, suicidal thoughts entered my brains, regrets of relationships and neglected myself, but I managed to let go and let God fix this mess. I kneeled with head bowed, and shoulders slumped, giving my all as I poured out, tears of pain, and turned into tears of joy as I was alive once again. I saved myself because I believed and I walked with faith and not by sight. I believed that my spiritual journey began in its perfect time. I did hit rock bottom, but I survived and I thank my higher power each and every day for saving my life. I've been healed by the power of my voice, I spoke it into existence and believed that positivity brings fourth life.

ABOUT THE AUTHOR

My name is Darshini Devi Ramsaran, age thirty five, born in Georgetown Guyana, raised in Brooklyn, East New York since the year of 1993. I am a Virgo, Optimistic, caring, loving, loyal and a social butterfly. I enjoy reading, writing, singing, crocheting, arts and crafts, drawing, and helping others. My mother Mohanie Ramsaran was born and raised in Georgetown, Guyana and my father Mahadeo Ramsaran was born and raised in Tunapuna, Trinidad. I have Three brothers, two eldest which are, Seunauth Deonarain, Hansraj Deonarain and one younger brother, Satish Ramsaran. I am the only female child, among four children. I came from a home filled with love, compassion, and strength. I am a rape victim who have overcame and currently overcoming each waking day. My message to the universe is that no matter what challenges we may face in life, do not lose hope, faith and love. The world is brutal but faith, hope and love always win.

Made in the USA
Columbia, SC
08 April 2021